MOB TOWN 251

**Lock Down Publications and Ca$h
Presents**

Mob Town 251
A Novel by *Von Diesel*

Lock Down Publications
P.O. Box 944
Stockbridge, Ga 30281
www.lockdownpublications.com

Copyright 2021 by Von Diesel
Mob Town 251

First Edition May 2021
Printed in the United States of America

This is a work of fiction. Names, characters, places, and incidents either are products of the author's imagination or are used fictitiously. Any similarity to actual events or locales or persons, living or dead, is entirely coincidental.

Lock Down Publications
Like our page on Facebook: Lock Down Publications @
www.facebook.com/lockdownpublications.ldp
Cover design and layout by: **Dynasty Cover Me**
Book interior design by: **Shawn Walker**
Edited by: **Nuel Uyi**

Stay Connected with Us!

Text **LOCKDOWN** to 22828 to stay up-to-date with new releases, sneak peaks, contests and more...

Thank you!

Submission Guideline.

Submit the first three chapters of your completed manuscript to ldpsubmissions@gmail.com, subject line: Your book's title. The manuscript must be in a .doc file and sent as an attachment. Document should be in Times New Roman, double spaced and in size 12 font. Also, provide your synopsis and full contact information. If sending multiple submissions, they must each be in a separate email.

Have a story but no way to send it electronically? You can still submit to LDP/Ca$h Presents. Send in the first three chapters, written or typed, of your completed manuscript to:

LDP: Submissions Dept
P.O. Box 944
Stockbridge, Ga 30281

DO NOT send original manuscript. Must be a duplicate.

Provide your synopsis and a cover letter containing your full contact information.

Thanks for considering LDP and Ca$h Presents.

CHAPTER ONE

Keith Monet sat comfortably behind his huge, solid oak desk with his feet propped up, staring out of his office window. He sipped on a tall glass of iced tea while he watched a beautiful young woman browse through rows of cars. She seemed to be giving the most of her attention to a white 2020 Ford Mustang.

The dropped top was what grabbed her attention. That, he was sure of. That's why he let it down when he got to work that morning. He knew that convertibles were young women's first choice. With the top down, they could be seen while they paraded up and down the streets going nowhere. He also knew that it was income tax time and they would be flocking in, trying to spend their tax returns before they even got them.

It was only his third year working at the dealership, and he had already been promoted to top salesman. He was good at what he did and took pride in his work. Keith hustled cars like a dope man hustled dope. He was young, tall and extremely handsome. A highly intelligent young man, most would say. That, alone with his charm and wit, helped him earn an enormous commission check every month.

He could wheel and deal anybody, but he preferred doing business with women. They were just as easy to talk out of their money as they were their panties.

He wasn't a star but he was very well known around Mobile. His name was brought up in every beauty salon, nail shop, club and everywhere else females hung out in the city. He was a player at heart and they all knew it. But yet and still, they couldn't get enough of the young stud. He could trick them into doing damn near anything he wanted, without effort. His friends tried to mock his style, but couldn't come close. Like he informed them a long time ago, he was a pimp by nature, not by choice. And that, he truly believed.

Keith hated the way men were today. They bought pussy. They constantly wined and dined women, making it bad for all the real players out there. He thought God made woman for a man, not man for a woman, and it was man around whom the world revolved.

If women could get paid just by lying down and opening up their legs, then surely a man could be paid for doing all the work. In his book, there wasn't a pussy out there that was worth more than his dick.

There was a knock on the door.

"Come in," Keith said without taking his eyes off the young woman out front. For a second, he got a brief peek at her panties as she bent over to pick up something she dropped.

His co-worker and closest friend, Devontae, came through the door carrying two boxes of Popeye's chicken. He tossed one of the boxes onto Keith's desk. Keith picked the box up and opened it. He frowned at its contents.

"What the fuck is this?" Keith asked. "I told you to bring me two legs, a breast and a pepper. I see two legs and a damn thigh." Keith frowned.

"Why every time you speak to me, you have to yell and shit? You ain't got to talk to me like I'm stupid."

"The hell I don't," Keith snapped. "You've got to start paying more attention to shit, Devontae, man." He shook his head in disgust. He hated thighs, and he couldn't eat nobody's chicken without a pepper.

"Nigga, you act like you my damn daddy or something." Devontae was twenty-four, three years younger than Keith.

"Sometimes I feel like I am your daddy, nigga." He took a leg out of the box, placing it on a napkin. He reached over, opening up Keith's box. Without asking, he took out his pepper. "Since you forgot mine, I'm taking yours."

Keith brushed it off. Arguing with Devontae could turn into an all day thing if he let it. Devontae was a light-skinned dude with short, wavy hair and big, brown eyes. He used to fall in love quickly and was easily suckered by girls, until he and Keith started hanging out. Keith made him tighten up his game and realize how much of a stud he could be. He already had the body and the brown eyes, he just needed the game.

Finally, Devontae sat down in one of the two chairs in front of Keith's desk. "You got a fucked up attitude, Keith. You know that? Next time, just go get the shit yourself. That way you ain't got to worry about me fuckin' up your order." He took a piece of chicken out of his box. "You act like people can't make mistakes."

"You said that like it was your first time or something." Keith responded. Keith noticed that Devontae had sat down. "Who the fuck said you could eat in my office?"

Devontae stared at him in disbelief. Keith could be an asshole sometimes over the pettiest shit. "Man, fuck you," Devontae stated. "I can eat in here if I want to."

"I can eat in here if I want to," Keith mocked him. "You sound like a little bitch."

"Yeah, whatever."

"Keith chewed on a leg while focusing his attention back on the girl outside. Now she was sitting behind the wheel inside the Mustang, pretending to be driving. Devontae said, "Why don't you take your cranky ass out there and sell a car or something."

Keith shook his head. "She ain't ready yet," he said evenly. He seemed to have calmed down.

"So what happened with that bitch you left the club with last night?" Devontae asked, changing the subject.

"I fucked her," he replied nonchalantly. "Fuck you think happened?"

"That bitch was bad. Pussy was good, wasn't it?'

Keith shrugged. "You've fucked one, you've fucked them all."

"That reminds me," Devontae said, reaching for his cell phone. "Heather is supposed to buy me this watch on Thursday." He showed him a picture he had stored in his phone. "She says she wants me to have something to remind me of her. She got one just like it."

Keith shot accusing eyes at him. "Y'all been spending an awful lot of time together lately," he complained. "You sure you ain't falling in love with that bitch?" He said "bitch" just to see how Devontae would react.

"Hell naw. She's just cool," he said weakly. He knew why Keith had called her a bitch. He wasn't gonna give him the satisfaction by commenting on it.

"Good." Keith sat up in his chair. "Let the bitch fall for you, man. Every woman is a fool for pretty niggas like us. They'd suck our shit through a straw if they could." He pointed a finger at him. "Take advantage while you can. You'll be having to buy pussy after you turn fifty."

"I thought you said you would never buy no pussy."

"I ain't. That's why I said you'll have to."

Devontae wiped his hands with a napkin. "If I got to buy it, then I don't need it."

Keith smiled as he stood up, stretching his long frame. Once again, Devontae had passed his verbal test. He patted him on top of his head. "Just making sure you're still on point, bro," he said on his way out the door.

The thought of a woman tricking for Devontae tickled Keith. He could remember when Devontae was too scared to ask a girl for some pussy, let alone some money.

Keith walked outside to approach the young lady. "How are you today?" he asked, thrusting his hand forward. "My name is Keith Monet."

"I'm fine," she replied sweetly. She was still sitting behind the wheel of the car.

"Yes, you are," he flirted. "What can I do for you today?" He put his hands inside his pockets and leaned up against the car.

She looked up at him through soft, worried green eyes. He knew right away what that look meant: I want this car, but I don't have enough credit. He had a remedy for women in her situation.

"I am so in love with this car." She toyed with the wheel like a child. "But the price--"

"Too high, huh?" he said, cutting her off.

"Mmm hmm," she grunted.

"What's your name?"

"Kylie," she said with a smile. Her mother taught her to always keep a flirtatious smile on her face when buying anything from a man. Sometimes it works, sometimes it doesn't.

"Kylie," he repeated. "Have you ever had a credit check done?"

"Yes, but they only approved me for a twenty-thousand dollar loan, and I only have a thousand to put down."

"Hmm?" Keith took a moment to think to himself. "There might be something that I can do for you. Follow me inside."

"Okay, she said happily." He opened the car door for her.

The smell of his cologne and the way that he looked in his Armani suit turned her on. She knew he had his way with women. She had heard of Keith Monet long before she met him. He was real smooth. The kind of guy she would like to get next to. It would be refreshing to date someone different than the drug dealing thugs she was used to.

Keith rid his office of Devontae and told Kylie to have a seat.

"Do you mind if I call you K'Mo?" she asked. She shot him a seductive look. "That's what all the girls down at the shop call you. I think that's a sexy-ass name."

She's trying to run a game on me, he thought. I knew she didn't think that lame shit is gonna work on me. I can't get mad at her for trying, though.

He took a seat behind his desk, trying to suppress his smile. "Call me whatever makes you feel comfortable." He stared into her eyes.

She blushed, wanting to look away, but couldn't seem to take her eyes off of him. He was fine as a mothafucka. She thought she was being admired, but she wasn't. He was searching her face for weakness and vulnerability.

Satisfied with what he saw, he pulled out a tan folder from his file cabinet.

"It says here that the Mustang is going for twenty-six thousand dollars." He closed the folder, setting it down on the desk. "And you say that the bank only approved you for a twenty-thousand-dollar loan?"

"Mm hmm," she said nervously.

He leaned back in his leather chair." Well, I do have a special program for women in your situation. But it's--

"I know all about your program," she blurted back.

Now he knew why she was wearing that short skirt.

"Aw, yeah? How do you know about that?" he asked suspiciously.

"My friend, Shauntie," she replied proudly. She works at the beauty shop down on Broad. She told me what you did for her. That's why I came to see you."

Shauntie, he thought to himself. Yes, he remembered her well. After selling her a new Mustang, he ended up spending the whole weekend with her. They had checked into a hotel that Friday and didn't come out until Monday morning. Her pussy was worth what he had done for her.

"K'Mo," Kylie called out, bringing him back to reality.

"Huh? Yeah, I remember Shauntie. She's the one with the tongue ring, right?"

She nodded. "Yeah that's her."

"Alright, then." He took a sheet of paper from his desk drawer. It was a contract. He handed it to her.

It read:

I, _____, agree to pay Keith Monet, the amount of five thousand dollars in twenty-five monthly payments of two hundred dollars.

Her face balled up after she finished reading it.

"What's this for?" she quizzed. "Why do I have to pay after we do what we're gonna do?"

His eyebrows shot up, "Look here, baby, I mean, I'm sure your pussy is gold and all, but it ain't worth no five grand."

"Shauntie said that all I had to do was fuck you, and you'd hook me up."

"Shauntie told you right." He sat up in his chair. "Look at it this way, baby. I'ma give you a pre-approved five-thousand-dollar loan, with only a shot of pussy as an interest fee. You can't beat that."

12

"Just a shot of pussy," she repeated. "You said that like I'm some type of ho or something. I ain't no damn ho nigga."

He sighed. "Look here, I didn't call you no ho, but if you want this car bad enough, you're gonna have to temporarily stoop to the level of a ho to get it." He turned around, pointing out the window. "I've got a whole selection of raggedy ass cars out there that you could easily get approved for."

She pictured herself pulling up to the beauty shop in her sporty new drop top Mustang. All them hoes would hate on her. And don't let her put some 17" chrome rims on it. Suddenly, she didn't care what she had to do to get it.

"Fine, she said hastily. "Let's get this over with."

He got up, slowly walked over to the door, and opened it up.

"What are you doing?" she said curiously.

"I've changed my mind," he said calmly.

"Why?"

"Because your attitude is not acceptable up in here. I'd rather just say fuck it, altogether."

She stood up and walked toward the door. She placed her hand on top of his, removing it from around the doorknob. She closed the door. "I'm sorry," she pleaded, still holding his hand. "Shauntie just didn't tell me all of the details. I'm cool with it."

"You sure?"

"Mm hmm." She leaned forward, kissing him and backing him up toward his desk.

He broke away from her so he could pull the shades on the windows. Then he took a Magnum condom out of his desk drawer. He pulled her close to him and backed her up toward his desk.

He broke away from her so he could pull the shades on the windows. Then he took a Magnum condom out of his desk drawer. He pulled her close to him and started kissing on her neck. Carefully, he slid her skirt down to the floor while she fumbled with his zipper.

While he put on the rubber, Kylie bent over and placed her hands flat on his desk. Reaching back behind her butt, she pulled her panties to the side.

13

"Fuck that shit," Keith said when he saw what she was doing. He pulled her panties down to her ankles, spread her butt cheeks, and then entered her.

"Ummmmph," she moaned as her lips parted.

He started with slow, shallow strokes until she loosened up. After a while she began to meet him pound for pound. He proceeded to punish her, banging her head against the computer.

Devontae and one of his white co-workers, Jason, were walking past Keith's office when they heard Kylie's muffled moans coming from the other side of the door.

"You hear that, man?" Jason asked, stopping in his tracks.

"Hear what?" Devontae replied, playing stupid.

"That moaning sound coming from Keith's office?" He walked up to the door.

"Why don't you mind your own business sometime? That's the problem with white people today. They always got their noses in somebody else's business."

"Chill, man." Jason put his ear up against the door. "Sounds like he's in their fuckin.'"

Devontae grabbed him by the arm. "Mind your business. Now come on, we've got customers outside."

"Keith is a fuckin' black stud, man," Jason said on their way outside.

Devontae shook his head, thinking about how careless Keith was getting. He was in his office fucking her hard like he was at home. He was gonna fuck around and get them both fired and thrown in jail.

Keith's mouth dropped open when he began to ejaculate. Grabbing her ass, he continued to thrust harder, until the last drop was expelled. He carefully pulled off the rubber and tossed it into the trash. After he pulled up his pants, he dropped down in his chair, panting and sweating. They were both out of breath. "Goddamn, girl! You a beast," he managed to say in between breaths.

She smiled, feeling proud of herself. You wasn't a bad fuck yourself, she thought as she slipped back into her skirt. After that,

14

the thought of her degrading herself for the car disappeared from her mind.

Finally, he collected himself. He called the service manager and told him that the Mustang convertible in the front row was sold. He watched as the car was being driven away to be washed and gassed up. It was time to get down to business. He notarized the contract after she signed it. Then he finished the remaining paperwork.

"Can I have my keys now?" She was brushing wrinkles out of her skirt.

"Just a minute." He was busy writing. "I'm gonna need your down payment and proof of insurance." He looked up at her.

She reached into her purse and pulled out a Geico insurance card. "All I have to do is call this number after I get your approval. This is the same company that insures my mama's car." Taking out her wallet, she pulled out a stack of bills, counted out one thousand dollars, then handed it to him.

He counted it twice before pocketing it. "What's the name of your bank and loan officer?" She gave it to him, then he made the necessary calls and things were done.

He grabbed a set of keys off a rack on the wall and handed them to her, along with a receipt.

"That'll do it," he said, clapping his hands together. "Take the paperwork over to your bank. Oh, yeah," he reached into his shirt pocket, took out his business card and handed it to her. "Send my payments to that address." The card had his home address on it.

Kylie twirled the keys around in her hand like an anxious child. "Okay. Is that it?"

"Yep."

She was headed out the door when the service manager returned with the car. She stopped and turned back around. "Can I call you sometime?"

"Please do."

She smiled. "I think I will. Don't let this little episode taint what we could probably become in the future. Okay? Because I'm really a good girl."

"I promise I won't."

"Bye," she said with a short wave of her small hand.

Keith was standing in the parking lot, waving her off, when his boss walked up, "Mr. Morris. How you doing?" he said with a smile.

Mr. Morris was old and tall with a head full of white hair. He was about his business and rich, but he was still a down-to-earth kind of guy. He pointed a crooked finger at the trunk of the leaving Mustang.

"I see you've sold that thing already."

"Yeah. I had to let her go for twenty-one thousand," he lied. Being that he was the head salesman, he was authorized to make such deals. Keith didn't have the authority to knock more than two grand off a price.

"That's good," Morris said, patting him on the back. "That's really good. Keep up the good work.

CHAPTER TWO

Keith clocked out at six o'clock. He hopped in his new Camaro and let the top down. It was a warm May day, so he removed his shirt and tie, revealing a white tank top that displayed his cuts. The big engine roared as it came to life. He spun his wheels on his way out of the lot.

When he pulled into the driveway of his Grandview home, he noticed that his garage window had been busted out.

"It had to be that bitch Natalie," he said out loud.

Natalie was his ghetto girl who loved to cause trouble when things weren't going her way. She paid well, so he didn't mind the lightweight drama.

He shook his head as he stepped over all the broken glass on his way inside. He turned off the alarm, threw his keys on the table, then pushed the play button on his voicemail. After he fixed himself a glass of Ciroc, he relaxed in his favorite recliner.

Message one: "Keith, this is Remy. I know you haven't forgotten about me already, playa. Anyway, I still want to take you out this weekend. Bye Bye."

Message two: "Keith, this is Natalie." she snickered. "I hope you're not mad about your broken window. You sho' don't mind breakin' hearts. Bye, pussy."

He frowned at the messages, shaking his head.

Message three: "What's up, nigga? This yo' boy Fabien. I hate to tell you this, but your bitch didn't make your car payment this month. Get with me so we can settle this matter.

Fabien was a long time friend of his who owned his own loan company. He gave Keith the loan for his Camaro after he promised not to miss a payment. Fabien was his friend, but business was business. Keith knew that if he didn't make the payment right away, it would be repossessed. Fabien didn't play games about his money, friend or no friend.

His business not being taken care of pissed Keith off. One of his women, Roseshell, was supposed to have paid his bill two days ago. She knew that it was an every month thing. What the hell is she tripping on? he wondered.

He dialed her number on his cell phone.

She picked up after two rings. "Hello?

"Shell," he said calmly. "How did you forget to make my car payment?"

For a moment, she was silent. "Hold on," she finally whispered.

He assumed that her wealthy lawyer husband was nearby. Ordinarily, he wouldn't have called her at home, but he wanted her to know how important this phone call was.

Keith had been dating Roseshell for over a year now. Secretly, he really liked her, but would never confess it even to himself. She was older, but still sexy, and cooler than any girl he had ever been with. She loved to lay up and spend time at his house, even though she had a husband at home. Keith made her feel good, young and still full of life, unlike her old stuck-up husband, Jermaine. She wasn't but thirty-five, but old in comparison to Keith.

Over time she had made a hobby out of buying Keith nice things. She loved to see him in the best, which is why she bought him the best. Roseshell didn't have to fantasize about these sexy models on TV and in GQ magazines. She had Keith. She made the payment on his car so he could look as good riding as he did walking. What did she care? It was Jermaine's money anyway.

"I'm back," she whispered into the phone. "I'm sorry baby, I---."

"Sorry don't pay my bills, baby," he said harshly. "You're the one who had me buy the damn car, now you don't want to make the payments."

"Baby, I said--."

"If you can't commit to your promise about a simple thing like this, how are you gonna commit to me one day?" He hung up the phone.

He laughed as he sipped on his Ciroc. She'd call back. She knew she had done wrong by not paying the bill on time.

Keith picked up his remote, turning on the flat screen TV that hung above the mantle. He was flipping through the channels when the phone rang.

Yeah."

"Keith," Roseshell pleaded.

"What?"

"I'm gonna take care of that first thing tomorrow, baby. I promise. I couldn't do it because Jermaine has been home sick all week. What kind of wife would I be if I weren't there for him?"

"He laughed. "What kind of wife cheats on her husband?"

"That's not fair, Keith. How could you talk to me like that?" Her voice was weakening.

He didn't let up. "If I'm the one you love, then I should be your first priority. I love you, but it's obviously a one way street.

"I love you too," she whispered. "And I'm sorry I let you down."

"Don't be sorry. Just take care of it," he demanded. "I'll talk to you later."

"You still mad at me?"

"How could I stay mad at you?" he said smoothly. "You're my boo. Now go take care of your sick husband."

"Bye, silly."

They hung up.

Later he'd check up on his other investors. He hoped that none of the others were late on their payments as well. Pam was in charge of his water bill, Melissa took care of the gas and Robin paid his light bill. The phone, cable and rent he could handle on his own.

His mother told him years ago that all women would be a fool for a fine man, in one way or another. At first, he thought she was just speaking of her own experience. However, as he got older, he believed what she told him was absolutely correct. But the one who wouldn't play the fool would be the one to consume his thoughts and actions. She would also be the one he craved daily, and would be the one he would want without a doubt.

CHAPTER THREE

Misty Munsey sat at a bar, sipping on a glass of Bacardi Limon. She bobbed her head slowly to the beat of the club's mixed jams. Men hovered around her, trying to get a close up of her big brown eyes. She didn't bite, instead, she played it cool, ignoring the lustful stares and corny pick-up lines that came at her.

She was there with the man she wanted to be with. In fact, he was one of the biggest ballers in Los Angeles. Even though she had only known him for three weeks, he had already told her most of his personal business. She knew how many bricks he was copping and that he had a house where he kept a half million stashed, in case he was ever kidnapped. All it took for her to get him talking was a couple of glasses of vodka mixed with cranberry juice. He hadn't even gotten the pussy yet.

He walked out of the restroom, wiping his hands with a paper towel. Her eyes were focused on him when he looked in her direction, meeting his gaze. With a nod of his head, he motioned for her to come over to him. She took a second to finish her drink. Flinging her curly black hair over her shoulders, she strutted over to where he was standing. Her black spaghetti-strapped cami and low cut capri jeans hugged her curves like they had painted on.

Misty was medium height, with olive-colored skin. She was slender, with a plump booty and shapely thighs and hips. She was Caucasian, but had the face of a Mariah Carey look alike.

Her hips swayed from side to side with the rhythm of the music as she neared him. He stood there with a player's grin on his face, checking out his young piece of game. Out of all the fish in the sea, he landed a whale when he caught her.

"What's up, Javaris?" she said in a low, sexy voice. She had a smile on her face that lit up the room. They were now standing body to body. Against her leg, she could feel a huge hump bulging out of his slacks.

"Hmm," she grunted, staring into his eyes. "Feels like you're workin' with a little somethin."

"Not a little somethin," he corrected her. He took her by the hand. "So are we gonna finally get down or what?

"Do you really want to?"

He let go of her hand and grabbed her waist, pulling her closer to him. "I want you to go to the hotel with me tonight," he said hopefully.

Misty frowned. "No, my first name ain't ho," and my last name ain't tel." She started rubbing her crotch up against his leg. "You got to take me to your crib if you want to get your groove on with me." She shot him a seductive look with her pretty browns to soften him up a bit. "If you don't trust me enough to take me to your house, that's cool," she said, flipping the script on him. "Trust me, I want to fuck you just as bad as you do me, but we can wait."

"It ain't like that," he lied. "I just thought you'd like it better if I took you to an expensive suite."

She began nibbling on his ear. "I want to see your bed," she whispered. She started caressing his zipper. "I want you to remember it every time you walk into your bedroom." She put his hand in between her legs.

"I guess we can do that," he agreed. His dick was hard, and he needed to release. What harm would it cause if he let her spend the night at his other house? He wouldn't take her where he laid his head, but he would take her to one of his stash houses to fuck the shit out of her.

They held hands while she followed him outside to his whip. He helped her into the passenger side, then quickly ran around to the driver's seat. Gently, she rubbed his leg and nibbled on his earlobe all the way to his house.

As soon as they got there, Javaris jumped into the shower while Misty made herself at home. The second she heard the shower come on, she immediately started snooping around the place. This was the house where he kept the ransom money stashed---she was sure of it.

Carefully and quietly, she rummaged through his bedroom drawers and closet and checked behind every closed door in the house. She came up with nothing but a gun, jewelry and expensive clothing. She gave up her search upstairs, and went to the basement door. It was locked with a padlock. Right then, she confirmed what she had already suspected. There was money in the house.

Misty flinched when she heard the running water stop flowing. Quickly, she hurried back to his bedroom and out of her clothes. When Misty walked into the room, she was stretched out, naked across his bed. Her small, olive-colored breasts were pointing straight up at the ceiling. He took a moment to admire her beauty. She motioned with her index finger for him to "come here." Slowly, he ran his eyes up her smooth legs all the way up to her chiseled stomach. Never in his life had he been with a girl who had abs.

Automatically her legs parted, inviting him inside her womb. With the skill of a man who'd slept with many women. Javaris stroked her gently while she slipped into a world of ecstasy.

Von Diesel

CHAPTER FOUR

Misty woke the next morning to the sounds of Javaris talking on the phone. The code talk that he was speaking let her know that he was handling business. Some of it she understood. Her knowledge came from years of dealing with guys who did illegal business for a living.

Goose bumps immediately covered her skin when she removed the covers from her naked body. Her eyes roamed the floor until she spotted her thong sitting on top of her jeans. She grabbed the rest of her clothes, pretending not to be listening to his conversation. He glanced over at her after he heard the bed springs squeak. Lowering his voice, he left the room, closing the door behind him.

Nigga, ain't nobody tryin' to listen to your conversation, she wanted to say, knowing damn well she was. She shook her head in disgust. After she finished showering and dressing, she went into the living room. Javaris was leaning up against his bar with the phone up to his ear. Now that there was light, Misty could see his slender, muscular physique. His abs flexed with each breath he took.

Javaris hung up the phone. "Morning baby," he said, placing his hands on her waist. "What's up for today?" He was in a cheerful mood.

"I've got to take my aunt somewhere," she lied. "So I won't be free until later on tonight."

He looked surprised. "Don't she got her own car?"

"Yeah, but she wants me to go with her." She removed her hands from her waist. "Don't worry baby, we gon' hook up later." She gave him a peck on his lips. "Just be patient."

"I love fuckin' you." he said seriously.

"Misty smiled. "Boy, don't talk to me like that." She smacked him gently on his shoulder. "You act like you been fuckin' me for years."

"I know. It was just so good last night, that I can't explain it. You'll never know the feeling of fuckin' a fine-ass woman like you."

"I should hope not," she replied. "You ready to take me home now?"

"Yep. Let me get my keys." He picked up his keys off the bar.

Her watchful eye noticed a small key on the ring that stood out from the rest. She figured it to be the key to the padlock that secured the basement door.

"What's that key for?" She pointed to it.

Javaris held the key ring up to his eyes. "It goes to a lock," he replied.

"What lock?"

The look he gave her told her that it was not something he wanted to discuss with her.

"Baby," she said. "You act like you got to keep everything secret from me." She fixed her pretty browns on him. "I'm down for you."

"You down for me?"

"Yeah. If a nigga try to get at you, he gon' have to go through me first."

That seemed to do the trick. "It goes to a lock on my basement door."

"Aww. You don't want nobody gettin' down there to your stash, I see." She put that out there just to see if he was gonna confirm or deny it.

"Somethin' like that," he told her, without leaking too much information. "You ready?"

"Yes."

When Javaris pulled up in front of Misty's aunt's house, he noticed some dude sitting in a new Dodge Charger, parked across the street. The guy was just sitting there, like he was waiting on somebody.

"Who dat?" he asked with a tinge of jealousy in his voice. This must be the reason why she needed to get home so fast, he thought.

26

"Who?" Misty said, looking at the car. "Oh, that's my cousin. He's smoking a blunt, probably. Auntie don't play that shit around her grandkids."

"Oh yeah?" He continued to watch the Charger.

"Come here," she said, pulling him toward her. "Give good-pussy Misty a kiss." She could see the unmistakably jealous look in his eye.

He finally shook it off, thinking that he was just paranoid. If that nigga is there for her, she wouldn't be trying to kiss me, he rationalized. He threw his arm around her neck, kissing her softly, for a long time.

"She placed her hand on his chest, pushing him away. "I gotta go now, baby." She grabbed her purse. "I'll see you later."

"Fo'sho."

She blew him a kiss after she exited the vehicle. Javaris sat there until she walked her sexy ass into the house. Turning around, she gave him one last wave before she disappeared inside. He smirked as he put his vehicle in gear. When he pulled off, he turned up the radio, blasting rap music from his high-dollar sound system.

Misty stood in the window, peeping through the mini blinds until Javaris was gone. After he was no longer in sight, she hurriedly jogged out the front door to the Charger parked across the street. She hopped into the passenger side, smiling from ear to ear.

"Hey love. I missed you," she said happily, hugging her boyfriend.

"Yeah, yeah, yeah," he grumbled. "You didn't miss me when he was nine inches up in you last night. Did you?"

Her smile faded. She regarded him curiously. "I did it for you." she reminded him. "Why you trippin'?" He didn't respond. With her arms folded across her chest, she shook her head and stared out the window. "I can't believe you, man."

KC could hear the sincerity in her vice and realized he was tripping. The girl sitting next to him loved him more than his own mother did.

"I'm sorry baby," he said in a sweet voice. He was trying to butter her up. Reaching out for her, he said. "Come here."

Misty resisted.

"No!" Get away from me!" she demanded, pushing him away. "You're a piece of shit. I'm out here risking catching AIDS, fuckin' all these niggas so we can have some money, and you worried about petty shit."

KC loved how pretty she looked when she was angry. Her high arched eyebrows pointed down at her cute little nose, like a devil. And he knew everything she said was true. He just wished there was a better way for her to trap their victims other than fucking them. It just wasn't right that half of the ballers in LA were getting some of his pussy.

"I said I was sorry, baby, damn," he pleaded. "You know how I am about you. "He took a freshly-rolled blunt out of the ashtray then fired it up. "So what's up with this nigga?" he asked with smoke flowing out of his nostrils.

She took the blunt out of his hand and hit it a few times. "He's a buster." she said, holding back a cough. She took another long hit, held it for a few seconds, then released the smoke into the air. "He's ready for the takin'."

"Cool," KC said. He then put the car into drive and pulled off. Misty rode in silence while KC contemplated their next move inside. "We gon' hit him tonight."

"Okay," she said humbly. Whatever he wanted to do, she went along with. He was the man and he knew best.

CHAPTER FIVE

Javaris walked out of the liquor store carrying a bottle of Remy Martin in one hand and a plastic cup full of ice in the other. He got into his whip, setting the bottle on the seat. His cell phone rang.

"Hello?" he said coolly.

"What's up, daddy?" Misty said. "When are you coming by? I'm feeling a little kinky right now."

Javaris popped the cork on the bottle, then slowly poured it over the ice. He took a sip before responding to her question. "I've got to make a quick stop somewhere first." He started his truck.

"Well, pick me up. I wanna ride, too." She sounded like a begging child. "Please don't leave me over my aunt's with all these bad-ass kids."

He thought about it as he pulled out of the parking lot into traffic. "A'ight. I'm on my way," he said with a big grin on his face.

He'd been with plenty of women, but something about this girl was different. He was happy to have her fine ass jockeying him like she was. But he made a promise to himself that he wouldn't let it go to his head.

Misty sat patiently, waiting on her aunt's front steps, entering the cool breeze that was blowing through her hair. Her eyes were fixed on a bird sitting on a tree branch making whistling noises, but her mind was on something else. She was hoping this would be a big enough score that she wouldn't have to go through this again.

Her plan was to get enough capital to open her own beauty shop, marry KC and live happily, but somewhere other than Mobile, Alabama. She had enough of the state and all the people who lived in it.

The loud thump of Javaris' music could be heard a block away. Misty snapped out of her trance and focused on what lay ahead of her. A dark blue Hummer came creeping down the street. It came to a stop in front of her house.

She smiled as she got up, dusting herself off. Slowly, she walked down the steps letting him get a good look at what she had to offer. She knew that she was eye candy. Her short sundress and matching bag went well with the color of her eyes. The leather sandals she wore showed off her white gold toe ring, which matched the choker around her neck. The soft wind blew her hair into her doll face. She stood there smiling coquettishly.

Javaris gazed at her candidly. They exchanged scorching looks. Finally, he got out of the truck and opened the passenger door to let her in.

"What's up, playa?" she said, getting into his truck.

"You, that's what's up." He got a gander of her pretty legs. "You lookin' good." he said lustfully.

"Thank you," she said shyly.

Javaris hopped into the driver's seat. She eyed the inside of the Hummer, impressed with its accommodations. It was fully loaded with soft, gray leather interior, a wooden steering wheel and a navigation system. He had a total of six TV screens inside the truck, including two in the headrests.

"Damn, your ride is tight," she complimented. "How much all of this cost?"

He smiled arrogantly. "I got over five grand into it," he said proudly.

"I wish I could afford something like this." She stroked his ego.

"That ain't no money for real. You should see the Excursion I got coming out this summer. I'm putting fourteen TV screens in that bitch."

"You rollin' like that?"

"And then some," he bragged.

Javaris whipped the Hummer into the parking lot of a McDonald's. He pulled over to a spot where a man was sitting parked in an old Monte Carlo SS. Javaris dug into his console and pulled out a Crown Royal bag. He glanced at his surroundings before he got out of the truck. Misty watched him get into the SS. From what she could see, it looked like they exchanged something. Five minutes hadn't gone by before he was back inside his own ride. She could see the lump of money that bulged out of his pocket.

That evening, they enjoyed a seven-course meal at a Japanese restaurant on Cedar Springs Road. Afterward, they rode arm in arm on a horse and carriage downtown Dallas around Klyde Warren Park. They spent the rest of the day enjoying each other's company. Javaris was a player. That, she couldn't deny.

It was getting late, they were feeling good and he was ready to feel her insides. He remembered how tight her pussy felt the night before and wondered how many men she had been with. She didn't seem like the type who slept around, but he could tell that she was experienced. No first-timer could work her pussy on a man like she worked hers on him.

He was used to having fine women around him, but Misty was in a class of her own. She was cool and real laid back, kind of like one of his partners or girlfriends. He wanted to tell Misty that he wanted her to be his "main thang," but he was afraid he would push her away by moving too fast.

Javaris cut off his headlights when he pulled into his driveway. With his hand on his gun, he eyed his surroundings carefully for anything suspicious. Shrubs, trees and darkness were all that he saw.

"What's wrong, baby?" Misty asked nervously. She was standing in front of the truck with her arms folded across her chest.

"Nothin'," he said, still looking around. "Just makin' sure ain't no punk-ass nigga waitin' around to jack me."

"Ain't nobody try to jack you while you're with me." She grabbed hold of his arm. "Let's go inside."

They were barely in the house when she dropped her bag onto the floor and attacked him. She kissed him roughly while she pulled the gun out of his pocket. He hadn't gotten a chance to lock the door before she was pulling him toward the bedroom. She pulled her dress over her head, then jumped into his arms. Javaris fell back onto the bed with her on top of him.

"Wait a minute, baby!" he said between their kisses. He pushed her off of him. "I gotta go lock the front door."

"In a minute, baby." She unbuttoned his jeans and pulled them down. He stepped out of them.

"I've got to do this now," he said seriously. He left the room. Misty sighed.

She needed the front door to be unlocked so KC could get in. Somehow, she'd have to get away from him so she could unlock the door again. Otherwise, she would have to wait until he fell asleep.

Javaris came back into the room and slapped his hands together. "Now, where were we?" He pulled her up close to him.

She pushed him on the bed. Kneeling down, she licked him from his feet, all the way up to his navel. She stopped suddenly.

He sat up frowning. "Wha' sup?" He had expected her to go down on him.

She put her finger up to her lips. "Shhh. I'll be back after I get some ice."

"Hurry up," he said impatiently.

Misty tiptoed to the front door while looking around to make sure he hadn't followed her. Quietly, she turned the lock until she heard it click. Opening the curtain, she peeked out for any signs of KC. He wasn't in sight. She picked up her bag off the floor and took out a small flashlight. She flashed it on and off in the window. Her body began to relax after she saw him flash his light back at her.

She put the flashlight back into her bag on her way to the kitchen. Javaris would be suspicious if she didn't come back with the ice. When she returned, he was still lying naked across the bed with his eyes closed. She grabbed hold of his organ and began to stroke it gently.

"Mmm...Did you get the ice, baby?" he asked without opening his eyes.

While his eyes remained closed, she eased a nickel-plated .38 out of her bag. She wanted him naked before she made her move.

Men seemed to get shy when they were naked. She wanted that advantage on him in case he tried to resist.

Javaris's eyes immediately popped open when he heard the hammer cock back. His mouth fell open as his eyes focused on the gun in her hand. Her arm twitched.

"Don't kill yourself," she said coldly.

"Kill myself? Bitch, you think I'm just gonna let you---? His voice trailed off after he saw KC enter the room. He fingered the trigger of the chrome Desert Eagle in his hand.

"Finish yo' sentence, nigga," KC said. He had a devilish grin on his face.

Javaris could tell by KC's composure that he'd done this before. Provoking him was not something that he was about to do.

KC reached down and grabbed Javaris's braided hair, snatching him off the bed. "Get yo' ass up!" Javaris got to his feet. KC looked at Misty. "Which way?"

She led them to the basement door. It was secured with the same lock she'd seen the day before. KC violently shoved Javaris into the door, telling him to open it. Javaris just stood there nervously, pretending that he didn't know what KC wanted him to do.

Whack! The side of the Desert Eagle came crashing down on Javaris's head. He felt the door, hollering, as blood ran down his face.

"Don't play dumb muthafucka!" KC yelled at him. "Open this muthafucka up!"

Misty stepped back out of the way, letting KC handle the situation. Javaris looked up at her with hate-filled eyes. How did I let this bitch make a fool out of me? he thought. Misty returned her own hateful stare back at him, unmoved by his cold look.

"I need the key," Javaris said, his eyes still fixed on Misty.

Why didn't I think of that before? Misty thought. She ran to the bedroom. Her hands were shaking while she searched his pants' pockets for the keys. She was ready to get the whole thing over with. She found them in his front pockets.

33

When she returned, Javaris was on his knees, shaking, as he was up close and personal with the barrel of KC's gun.

"I got 'em," she said, holding up the keys. She unlocked it herself.

Misty opened the door and KC shoved Javaris toward the steps. "Lead the way."

It was dark and clammy down there. It wasn't clean like upstairs. Javaris pulled a string and the room instantly lit up. A rat ran for cover behind the furnace. Javaris continued on, leading them behind the staircase.

Bolted into the concrete floor was a fireproof Sentry safe with an electronic lock. Javaris stood there like he didn't know what to do next.

"Fuck you waiting on? Open it up," KC demanded.

Javaris looked pleadingly at Misty again.

"What the fuck you keep looking at me for?" she yelled, irritated by his continued eye contact. She knew that he was looking for her to sympathize with him.

Javaris's stomach was in knots. He wasn't really tripping on the money. He had plenty of that stashed in houses all over town. His main concern was what was going to happen after he opened the safe.

KC became fed up with Javaris's stalling. He put the barrel flush up against the side of Javaris's head. "You gon' stand there, play games and end up dead? Or are you gonna open the damn safe? Last chance."

Javaris reluctantly pushed the correct numbers on the keypad. A green light flashed and the door popped open.

KC kicked Javaris out of the way. The sight of all that cash brought a tear to his eye. For years now they had searched for the perfect lick, and now Baby had finally struck gold. She bumped all the way to the top, KC thought greedily.

Javaris could tell by the crazed look in KC's eyes that he wasn't gonna let him live. He had to make a move soon if he wanted to get out there with his life.

KC took a trash bag out of his pocket. Eyes shining with pleasure, he said to Javaris, "I bet when you were stacking all of this money, you didn't know it was for me, did you?"

Javaris said nothing in return. He just stared at him. He watched KC stick his gun into his waistline. Misty had her gun drawn, but she was in striking distance. At that moment, she was keeping an eye on KC as he filled the bag.

While Misty was buty watching KC, Javaris made his move. He threw a quick, hard jab, hitting Misty in the side of her face. The gun flew out of her hand as she fell to the floor. KC turned from the safe, meeting a jab to his eye, then another to the side of his head. The bag dropped to the floor. He fell to his knees trying desperately to get his gun out.

Javaris jumped on him in an attempt to stop him. KC tried to poke his finger through Javaris' eye socket. Opening his mouth, Javaris big down on the side of KC's hand until he tasted blood.

Out of the corner of his eye, Javaris saw Misty recovering. She staggered over to her gun and picked it up off the floor. He let go of KC's hand and tried to rush her. The barrel of her gun was aimed toward his head. At that moment, he realized his life was over. His basement would be the last thing he would ever see.

Bam! Bam! Bam!

Misty fired three shots at his body. Blood splattered the safe, KC and the bag of money. She swallowed. Her stomach contracted into a tight ball as she realized what she had done. Usually, it was KC who carried out the killing part of their robberies. This time, the blood had been shed by her hands.

KC pushed the lifeless, bloody body off to the side. He stood up and slowly reached for the gun in her hand. She released it without incident.

"You did what you had to do, baby," he assured her. "Remember that."

Misty stared at the body like she had never seen one before.

"Come on, baby," he said. "Help me finish bagging the money."

After they finished, he ordered her to go to the police. They had a pre-fabricated story ready for the cops. Each of the robberies was carefully planned before it was put into effect. KC made sure that all angles were covered.

Or so he thought.

Misty ran up the stairs. On her way to the front door, her memory flashed back to the money that Javaris had gotten from the dude at the McDonald's. She made a quick detour to his bedroom. Inside his pants' pocket, opposite where she found the keys, she found the wad of money. She saw it when she was looking for his keys, but had been in too much of a hurry to grab it then.

She stuffed it inside her bag on the floor, then dashed out of the house. Intentionally, she ran through the shrubs so that she would get scratched up so it would look as though she hurt herself trying to get away. That, along with the knot that Javaris put above her eye, she thought should be convincing enough.

Searching for a way to dispose of the body, KC found a can of gasoline over by a riding lawn mower. He doused Javaris' body with the gas and ran a trail up the steps, all the way to the front door. He tossed the money bag over his shoulder, struck a match, threw it on the gasoline trail, then shut the door.

"Javaris' nosey white neighbor, Mr. Richards, saw KC running from the house. When he was long gone, she tiptoed over to Javaris' yard. That's when she saw the flames through a window.

"Jesus, Mary and Joseph!' she exclaimed. She turned and ran back to her house to call the police.

Damn near out of breath, Misty ran nonstop to the police station. She was huffing and puffing by the time she entered the building. "Help me! Somebody, please help me!" she hollered as she fell to the floor.

A heavyset black woman came running from behind the front desk. She kneeled down next to her. "Miss, are you alright?" she asked, helping Misty to her feet.

Misty took a second to catch her breath. "No. Some man just tried to kill me and my boyfriend."

The heavyset officer turned toward another uniformed officer who had just walked up. "Go get me Detective Ramos. Now!" The officer quickly ran to carry out the order.

Minutes later, she found herself sitting alone in a small room with a long conference table and six chairs. The heavyset office had gotten her a blanket and a cup of coffee while she waited to speak to the detective.

KC should have made it home safely by now, she thought. All of the evidence will be burned up, and we'll get off scot-free. She hoped this would be the last time she had to go through this, but if shit ever got back bad for them, she would gladly do it all over again.

She looked up nervously when the detective walked his tall frame through the door. He was dark as a human being could be with more gray hair on his head than black. Detective Ramos looked well over his forty-seven years.

He looked down at her through a set of old, experienced brown eyes. Still watching her carefully, he took out a pack of Kools and fired up a cigarette. She glanced over at the *No Smoking* sign on the wall, next to the door. She could already tell that he was a defiant asshole.

Ramos took a seat directly in front of her. Not a word was spoken. He just sat there, puffing on his cigarette.

"Why don't you tell me what you told Officer Jones," he finally said. He had a suspicious look in his eyes. Years of experience taught him to not always believe the first person's side of a story, especially when it was a woman telling it.

Misty wiped the fake tears from under her eyes.

"Me and my boyfriend were in bed, about to have...to have..."

"To have what?" Ramos interrupted.

"Sex," she said timidly.

"Umm hmm."

"Then somebody knocked on the door, and Javaris...Javaris got up to see who it was." She stopped, taking a moment to sob.

She was shocked that the detective never offered her a tissue or something to wipe her face with.

"...Well," she continued," I heard him in the doorway arguing with some guy about a girl or something. Anyway, I got up, slipped my dress back on, then went to see what was happening. That's when I saw Javaris strike the man in his face."

"What did you do then?" He was reading her eyes for a sign. If she looked to the left, then she was making up the story as she went along. If she looked to the right, then she was searching her memory bank.

Her eyes unexpectedly shifted to the right. She was searching her memory bank for the lie that she and KC had made up earlier that day. She continued. "I, umm, I ran toward them. That was when the guy kicked Javaris in the stomach and threw him against the wall. Then---"

"Where is your boyfriend now?" Ramos cut in.

Misty stood up, slamming her hand down hard on the table. "That's what I'm trying to tell you!" she yelled. I barely escaped. For all I know, that guy is still in the house. Javaris is probably...dead by now." She took deep, heaving breaths in between her sobs, making her words barely audible. She continued. "In the meantime, you're sitting here questioning me like---"

Ramos held his hands up for her to calm down. "We sent a car over to your boyfriend's. As soon as I---"

A short, white officer barged in, interrupting them. "Excuse me, sir," he said. "We just received a call from car number 211. He reported that the fire department was at her boyfriend's address when he arrived at the scene. It seems they think they might have found a body in the basement."

"Nooooo!" Misty cried out.

Ramos jumped up from the table. "You keep an eye on her," he ordered. "I'm going over to that address."

CHAPTER SIX

"Let me speak to P'Cola," Keith said into his cell phone. The sun was out and he had the top down on his Camaro, rolling down Government Boulevard.

"Who dis?" P'Cola asked, answering the phone.

"This Keith, nigga. How many heads you got up there?" He hit his signal and changed lanes, pressing the gas to pass a slow-moving minivan.

"One, two." He could hear P'Cola counting heads in the background. "I've got about two people in front of you," P'Cola said. "What you gone do?"

"I'm on my way down there now. All I need is a fresh taper with a razor line."

"Bring ya ass, trick daddy." P'Cola laughed at his own humor.

"On my way." He turned up the volume on his radio, bumping Miguel's, *Real Ass Nigga.*

P'Cola's Barber & Beauty was located on the south end of Mobile, Alabama. For his skills, you had to pay twenty dollars for a regular haircut and twenty-five for a style. P'Cola honestly felt that he belonged in Hollywood or on the East Coast, cutting stars' heads, like Ice-Cube. He felt everybody in Mobile whose hair he cut should consider themselves privileged to have him at their disposal for only twenty-five dollars. They could always go to *Cut Em' Up* down the street and only pay fifteen.

All of the latest news, like who's got the dope, who's fucking who and even who shot who, could be found out there. All you had to do was sit for a while.

Keith liked it there because of the fine-ass hoes who hung out in the beauty shop. The place was decked out with a pool table in the back, two TVs with a PlayStation 4 and an Xbox.

P'Cola looked up from cutting some dark-skinned dude's head just as Keith walked in. He wore heavy, starched Red Monkey shorts, a white wife beater and white Air Force Maxes.

"Trick, what's up?" P'Cola cut off the clippers and shook P'Cola's hand.

P'Cola stood just as tall as Keith, but with a wider frame. He wore an Alabama Crimson Tide baseball cap, tilted to the left over his braided hair. P'Cola was a shit-talking muh-fucka. Everybody was a trick to P'Cola, except for P'Cola. He was cool with everybody, but if he was ever crossed, he could be as treacherous as a bitch with a broken heart.

"Y'all packed up in here," Keith said, glancing around the room at the crowd of women looking through magazines and sitting with their heads under dryers.

He caught a glimpse of one of the beauticians. Kathea, eyeing him. He winked at her as he took a seat in front of P'Cola's chair.

P'Cola started cutting on Dark Skin's hair again. Lil' Ant was the barber whose chair was next to P'Cola's. Peeping through his gold-framed spectacles, Lil' Ant masterfully cut away on a brown-skinned guy's head.

"What you been up to Keith?" Lil' Ant asked without taking his eye off of his customer.

"Not a damn thing," Keith said, picking up a GQ magazine.

Brown Skin said, "Like I was saying, Ant. So I'm fucking' this bitch, right? She's screamin' and hollering like a muh-fucker. I spit the first nut out quick. Like bam!" He snapped his fingers.

"Uh huh," Lil Ant said, lining up the back of his head.

"So, I keep on humping like I haven't cum yet. Man, you know what that ho said to me?

Nigga, get that limp thing outta me," he said, imitating a woman's voice. "And the bitch got up, too. I was embarrassed like a muh-fucker."

Everybody inside the shop laughed.

Kathea stopped rinsing some girl's head and said, "You should have popped a Viagra." She laughed along with everybody else.

"P'Cola said, "Man, I'm so sick of you and these stories about you' ole no-good ass tramps."

Lil' Ant smiled, showing four solid platinum teeth. "Me too. They don't even be funny." He snatched the cape off of the dude. "Get yo-dry-joke-telling ass up."

Keith waited until P'Cola finished with Dark Skin's head, then he got into the chair.

"Nigga, sometimes I swear you're sellin' dope." P Cola popped the cape in the air, knocking the hair off. He was referring to the huge diamond earrings that were in Keith's ears.

"Sellin' a lot of cars, man," Keith said proudly.

"Yeah, I heard about that scam you and Devontae got going on up there."

Keith just smiled.

He remained still while P'Cola went to work on his wavy head. An older man was standing over his son in Lil' Ant's chair, telling the boy to hold still. For a minute, Keith wished that he had a son to take to the barber with him. But for him, there was just too much that came along with being a father. All the baby mama drama and whatnot.

A tall, thick girl with dreads walked into the door. "What's up y'all. Hi, Keith." She had on a too big Nike T-shirt and denim blue jean shorts, that hung to her knees. She carried her barber's bag over to her chair and began setting up her clippers.

"Hey, babe," Keith mumbled, barely moving his lips, while P'Cola trimmed his goatee.

Star was what a dyke would call a "stud." She was the dominant female in her lesbian relationships. Keith often wondered what it would feel like to be inside of her tight womb gate. She was a butch, but a fine one, with her chocolate ass.

"Star!" a tall redbone chick with long, burgundy-colored hair yelled from the doorway. "You forgot your cell phone, baby."

Her tight ass jiggled as she swayed over to where Star was standing. Star took the phone and gave her a wet "thank you" kiss on the lips. All she was doing was putting on a show for the people inside the shop.

"Thank you, baby," Star said smoothly.

"I'll be back to get you 'round six." Redbone said as she turned to leave.

P'Cola's oldest customer, Junebug, stopped reading his newspaper just to get a good look at the young tender.

41

"Lawd have mercy." He shook his head. "If I was twenty years younger, I'd have to have me a taste of that."

P'Cola chuckled. "Junebug, you say that about every broad who comes through that door, and I ain't seen you pull up on one of them hoes yet."

"He scared," Lil' Ant added.

Junebug frowned. "I bet you I pull mo' hoes in that eighty-three Fleetwood I got outside than you do in yo' new Tahoe," he said defensively.

"Shiiid!" Lil' Aint retorted. "You see how many different hoes I got running in and out of here?" He moved his short, thick frame to the front of his chair, dusting the excess hair off the boy's head.

A man with a box-style haircut stood up and looked out the window, stalking Redbone as she walked to her car.

"I know Star's suckin' the shit outta that pussy," he said a little too loudly.

"What you say?" Star said angrily. She set down her scissors.

The man glanced around the room like he didn't know who she was talking to. "Huh? I didn't say nuthin' to you."

"Yes, you did, nigga," she said, moving closer to him. She put a finger up in his face. "Yo' bitch ass probably want me to suck yo' pussy, Pussy."

"Bitch, you got me fucked up," he said defensively. His bumpy face hardened. "Better get the fuck outta my face."

Her eyes sharpened. She looked at him like she was about to swing on him at any second.

"Blue," P'Cola called out. "Sit your ass down."

Blue's face balled up. "Naw, man. She ain't gonna get away with calling me no pussy up in here."

P'Cola cut off his clippers and walked over to Blue. "I promise you don't wanna start no trouble up in here. Better yet, get yo' ass up outta here. Come back tomorrow."

Blue grimaced. "Yeah, okay," he said, inching toward the door. P'Cola walked back over to his station, shaking his head. "Star, you gotta stop gettin' into it with everybody. Damn, I know you're a butch ass dyke and all, but sometimes you have to let shit go. You gettin' bad for business.

"He started it, P'Cola," she whined, watching P'Cola dust the hair of Keith's neck.

P'Cola ignored her.

Keith heard loud music coming from outside, shaking the windows. He waved to everybody as he headed for the door.

"Hold on a minute, Keith, I'ma walk out with you." P'Cola took off his apron.

Junebug looked up at Lil' Ant. "Just for the record," he said, "them girls you got runnin' in and out of here--don't none of 'em look like shit, except for your woman."

Lil' Ant smirked. "Go 'head on, Junebug."

A black Range pulled up behind Keith's Camaro. Fabien hopped his short, muscular frame out of the SUV. He sported a white tee, True Religion jeans and red and black Air Force 1's.

They all shook hands. "I knew I'd find yo' ass up in here," Fabien said to Keith. "Wha' sup wit' it, P'Cola?"

"Shid...a gorilla," he bragged. "Aw, yeah, I saw yo' bitch Shaquilla today.

"Where at?"

"She was up at Mudbugs." He was referring to a local fish joint. "Bitch was lookin' good as a muthafucka."

"She get that money to you?"

"Mm hm. I started to get on her fine ass. See how tight your game really is." Fabien backed away from his smiling. Six platinum and diamond teeth blinged between his lips.

Keith looked at him doubtfully. "It wouldn't have done you no good. When I got a bitch, I got a bitch," he said arrogantly.

P'Cola brushed him off. "Ole trick-ass nigga, please. If you was paying me, I wouldn't fuck with nobody else either." He and Fabien chuckled.

"You better ask Fabien about me, man. Keith Monet ain't never paid a ho."

"Damn, Fabien. You ain't got no greens?" P'Cola asked.

"Unt unh."

"Yuna and Usher's "Crush," was beating out of a black, chromed out Chrysler 300. They watched lustfully as the caramel-colored, blond-headed woman parked in front of the shop.

She stepped out, sporting yellow shades and a short, tight yellow tennis skirt. She slung her Coach bag over her shoulder as she headed toward them.

"Who's that?" Keith asked, licking his lips.

The tall, leggy woman walked past Fabien and Keith both, stopping in front of P'Cola.

"Hey daddy," she said sweetly.

P'Cola remained in player mode while his boys were around. "Wha' sup baby? You should've been here an hour ago." He glanced at his watch. "My lunch break is over now," he complained.

"Baby, you know I had to get my nails done." She held them up to the sub. "Jade had this new color that she wanted to try out. See." She put the florid-colored nails up to his face.

P'Cola saw Fabien and Keith eyeing him accusingly. He took her by the hand and said, "Let's go inside. We don't need our business all out in the streets."

"Take your trick ass inside then, "Fabien teased. "I bet' not ever hear you call nobody else a trick again."

"I ain't tryin' to hear it," he said, opening the door for her.

"We going to the *Gentlemen's Club* tonight or what?"

Keith shrugged. "I'm tired of fuckin' with the same run-down-ass hoes, man. We need to go where some fresh fish gon' be at. I'm tired of the same passive-ass bitches. I want to be where a bitch gon' shoot game right back at me."

"Call me and let me know what's up."

Fabien watched P'Cola disappear into the shop.

"That bitch got P'Cola by the balls," Fabien commented.

"I don't think so," Keith said doubtfully. "He's just kickin' it."

"What you about to do?"

"I'ma shoot around to mom's crib and check on them for a minute or two."

"Aight. I'ma get up with you later."

They headed in different directions.

Von Diesel

CHAPTER SEVEN

Marijuana smoke clouded the living room at Keith's mother's house. His daddy was sitting on the couch, dumping ashes into the ashtray, when Keith walked through the door. His daddy's friend, Wilbert Lee, was sitting on the love seat watching an old karate movie on TV.

"Hey, pops." Keith smacked him on top of his shoulders. His daddy looked at him like he was crazy through low, red eyes.

"How many times do I have to tell you to call me James, nigga? You can go on somewhere with that pop shit."

James was forty-four but looked and acted ten years younger. At least once a week, James had to curse Keith out about calling him "pops." James didn't take aging too well. There was no way that you could get him to believe that he wasn't still the shit.

Keith ignored James. "What's up, Wilbert Lee?"

"Shit, Wilbert Lee said in his loud, high-pitched voice.

Wilbert Lee was five feet, eleven inches tall and weighed over three hundred pounds. He had been James' closest friend since grade school. His only fault was that he told too many lies.

"I get any mail?" Keith shuffled through some mail on top of the fireplace.

"Mm hm," James said, holding in the weed smoke.

He stopped shuffling when he read the name Kebron Webster on an envelope. Kebron was his cousin who got caught up trying to rob a McDonalds three years ago. He was sentenced to twenty years in prison with no one to look out for him.

After hearing all the stories about his uncle's experiences in the joint, Keith couldn't let his cousin be in there doing badly, so he made sure that he set aside three hundred dollars a month to send to Kebron and visited him when he could.

Keith stood there reading the letter from Kebron, which told him about everything that was going on on the inside. And of course, he needed some more money. As fast as Kebron's going through money, he has to be gambling, Keith thought. Kebron had a nasty gambling habit, but never won as long as Keith had known him.

Back when they were in high school, they used to shoot dice in the boys' restroom. Kebron would lose his money quickly, before the late bell rang. Still, you would see him back the next day trying his luck. Keith suggested that Kebron stop rolling the dice and start betting on whoever was winning. When he tried that, the boy who was winning, stopped winning. Talk about bad luck.

Keith balled up the letter on the way to the kitchen where his mother was. She was standing over a pot of greens cooking on the stove.

"Mmm," Keith said, sniffing the aroma. "What you cookin', baby?"

"Collard greens and ham hocks." She gave him a confused look. "Since when did greens start smelling good to you?'

"When I grew up." He kissed her on the forehead.

"Grew up?"

"That's what I said."

She shook her head. "You could've fooled me. Grown men have families and kids running around the house. Go to Cub Scout meetings and stuff like that. They don't run the streets, chasing whores all day."

"Whores?"

"Yes, whores." She turned down the fire on the stove, then faced him. With one hand on her hip, she said, "I know you don't call those tramps that you run around with women? I can't stand none of 'em. Especially Natalie's ghetto ass. Always trying to break up your shit." Her voice lowered. "I like Roseshell though. I think you should be with her. She has a lot going for herself."

"Got a lot going for herself? Mama, that's her husband's money. If you gon' call anybody a whore, it should be her."

She opened her mouth to say something, but words never came out. She was speechless.

"I guess she forgot to tell you that she was married during one of y'alls talks, huh?"

"Yes she did, but that's not my point." She was determined to hold her ground. "You need to slow your ass down, Keith. I don't want to wake up in the middle of the night to no phone call saying that somebody's husband done killed my baby." Her voice had taken on a seriousness that he understood completely.

They stared at each other in silence.

Finally, he cracked a smile, then gave her a hug.

Mama was almost as tall as Keith and very attractive. Like her husband, she too thought that she was still young and the shit. She had been through a lot in her forty-three years, and she'd seen what jealous boyfriends and husbands did to guys like her son. Keith being her only child, she would do anything to protect him.

"I'm gonna slow down, mama. I promise," he lied. "Just as soon as you stop going out to clubs," he said, then quickly left the kitchen.

"I go out with my husband, thank you," she hollered at his back.

Keith took a seat next to James on the couch. He was thinking about what his mother had just told him. What if some hating-ass nigga did try to kill me over they girl? Would Roseshell's husband try some shit like that? You never can tell. I've got to be more careful and tighten up my game before some shit like that does happen.

James saw the distant look on his son's face.

"What's up, son? Some girl got you feeling down or something?" James giggled. "Look like you done lost your best friend."

"I know," Wilbert Lee agreed. He noticed the distant look on Keith's face also. "You alright, little nigga?"

Keith frowned. "Ain't nothing wrong with me. I'm just thinking."

"Well go somewhere else and think," James said. "Don't come up in here blowin' my high." He thumped ashes into the tray. "Wilbert Lee, man, I wouldn't want to be twenty-four again for nothing in the world," he chuckled.

"I know my dog ain't stressing over no broad," Wilbert Lee said.

"Yes he is. Young punk."

"Come on with all that shit, pops," Keith said. "Y'all know I'ma playa. Ain't nothing changed." He coughed from inhaling the weed smoke. "I was just thinking about something that mama said."

"Aw, shit," James said, passing the joint to Wilbert Lee. "Keep on listening to your mama, and you gon' always be fucked up." He fired up a Newport. "I used to keep your mama chasing me back when we were going to school."

"Sho' did," Wilbert Lee confirmed. "All the girls used to be on James. Remember when I fucked Savannah, what's her last name, starts with an "S" in that Johnny on the Spot, when we skipped school at Municipal Park?"

"No. Wilbert Lee, why is you lying, man? You ain't never fucked Savannah."

"Bullshit!" Wilbert Lee hollered. "That was the day we got that fifth of Thunderbird."

James shook his head while he puffed on the cigarette. "I remember the Thunderbird, but I don't remember you fucking nobody that day."

Keith laughed. He loved to hear his daddy talk shit to his friends. Sometimes he would talk about them so badly, they would get up and leave. But they would always return for the same treatment, and also to smoke up his weed.

Keith took out his wallet and counted out three hundred dollars. He placed it on top of the table. "Tell mama to send Kebron this money for me."

James asked, "How's he doing?"

Keith shrugged. "Same ole, same ole." He stood up. "I'ma holla at y'all."

***

"I want to spend the night with you, baby. Please!" Shani pleaded over the phone.

"I don't know, Shani," Keith replied. He rubbed lotion on his upper body. He had just stepped out of the shower and was preparing for the club. "I've gotta see what Devontae and Fabien is gonna do."

"So you're fuckin' Devontae and Fabien, now?" she said hotly.

"Come on with that bullshit." He sighed and shook his head. You can meet me at my crib around three forty-five, or so. I'ma leave the key under the mat. You already know my alarm code. If I'm not here when you get here, make me some breakfast."

"Okay, daddy," she said excitedly. He could imagine the smile on her face. "I'll be naked and ready to serve you."

"A'ight. "Peace."

"And please be drunk when you come home. Ya know how I like that drunk dick."

"Okay, but do me a favor."

"What?"

"Don't beg next time. Put your foot down."

"I'll never be too proud to beg for some of your dick, baby," she said proudly.

"I'll see you later." He hung up.

Admiring the way he looked in the full-Yak mirror, he could understand why Shani was feenin' so. "You's a sexy muthafucka, boy," he said to himself. "I don't know a bitch in her right mind who wouldn't want to be with you." The Armani suit hung just right on his muscular frame.

Reaching into his bottom drawer, he shuffled through four gold-framed portraits of each of his girls. He took out the one of Shani, then carried it to the living room and hung it up on the wall.

Satisfied, he picked up his phone and keys, set the alarm, then left the house.

Von Diesel

CHAPTER EIGHT

"Mmmm, Mmmm," Misty moaned softly while she was still asleep. She could feel a tingling sensation in between her legs. Slowly, her eyes fluttered open. Looking down, she saw the top of KC's wavy head. He was nibbling away at her pearl tongue.

"Unt unh. Baby, stop," she said softly, half enjoying it. She closed her legs in on his head. "We ain't got...mmm...time baby. I gotta go to work.

"Fuck work!" he said, trying to hold her legs open. "You don't have to work no more."

"Yes, I do. Now stop," she demanded, but it was no use.

Misty relaxed for a minute when she felt his tongue wagging around inside of her. She could feel herself becoming wetter by the second. Her legs went limp as she lay there in submission, waiting for him to let down his guard. Releasing the grip he had on her legs, he eased two fingers into her crevice. Then she made her move. In a swift motion, she swung her right leg over his head, rolled off the bed and stood up.

KC frowned at her with pussy juice around his mouth.

"What you doing?" he said hotly. He had been under the impression that she was enjoying it.

"I said no!" she hollered over her shoulder on her way to the bathroom.

His nature swelled as he watched her walk gracefully out of the room. She looked like a model going down the runway, naked. He sighed and sat up on the bed. The news was on TV. The anchor-woman was reporting a string of robberies that had taken place in Dallas/Ft. Worth. He had to laugh to himself, thinking about all the robberies he and Misty had gotten away with.

It was a shame how she could get so close to their victims so quickly. All it took was a pretty face and an hour in the sack. He couldn't figure out how some of them lasted in the game as long as they did when they were so gullible. He knew that he was damn lucky to have her like he did. She could've been with anybody she wanted. KC could see that by the way she worked their victims.

He got up and headed for the bathroom. Butt naked, she stood in front of the mirror and wrapped her hair into a bun. It went well with her doll face and slanted eyes.

KC eyed her curves lustfully. He wanted to stick dick to her bad to satisfy his morning hard-on, but he knew that she would not go for it. It was already after nine and she had to get to the beauty shop before her customers started showing up. Misty wasn't one to miss money. She had plans to open up her own shop one day soon. After the lick they pulled on Javaris, they had enough to do it now, if they wanted to.

Expensive trips to Bermuda, France and the Bahamas, and major shopping sprees in Southern California kept them from being able to keep any money in the past. Not to mention gambling in Vegas and dining in the fanciest restaurants in Atlanta. They treated themselves to the best, at other people's expense. This time it would be different. They'd invest their money into a legitimate business before their luck came to an end.

Misty cut her eyes at him. "You can lust, but you can't touch."

"I know," he said. "I can get off just by watching yo' fine ass."

"Well, that's what you're gonna have to do. Excuse me," she said, walking past him back into the bedroom.

She rubbed herself down with cocoa butter lotion. Then she squeezed into a pair of tight-fitting jeans and a pink blouse.

She wrinkled up her nose, smelling a foul odor in the air. She tried to ignore it, but the smell was getting worse.

"KC," she called out, "you shittin'?"

"Yeah," he grunted. That shit you cooked last night got my stomach fucked up."

Her lips curled up. "Aw, yeah?" Well next time don't eat that shit." She shook her head. "Damn, you can say some hurtful shit sometimes," she said angrily.

Hearing the toilet flush, she grabbed her keys and purse, then stormed out of the room before he had a chance to apologize. She knew that he meant every word that he said. She had just opened the front door when he came running down the stairs.

"Hold on, boo boo," he pleaded. He reached around her, pushing the door closed.

She folded her arms across her chest. "What, boy?"

"What you mean, what? Girl, you know I was just talkin' shit. You gettin' mad over nothin'."

"Because you always sayin' shit to put me down. Then you try to apologize. You know damn well that I'm sensitive about my cookin'." She grunted. "I don't say nothin' about you droolin' all over the pillows and shit at night."

"I don't say nothin' about you being a ho," he said defensively, "round here fuckin' everybody but me."

"I have to ho around so we can have some money around this muthafucka," she said, bobbing her head. "Something your trifling ass can't seem to get on your own.

He looked at her furtively. "Don't act like you don't enjoy it."

She reached around him and opened the door. "That's it. I ain't got to take this shit." She faced him. "And don't try to apologize later." She stormed out the door. Impotent muthafucka, she thought to herself.

"Leave then, bitch," he mumbled under his breath. "I got all the money."

***

Misty arrived at the beauty shop fifteen minutes late. Tiffany and Evelyn were sitting in the waiting area, flipping through magazines, looking pissed off. They had other things to do besides wait on her all day.

"I know Misty Munsey ain't late for work," Evelyn said sarcastically." Miss Thang ain't never late."

Tiffany had no time for games that morning. "Misty, you know that I gotta be at the airport by one," Tiffany complained while she followed Misty to the bowl.

Misty sighed. She put her hand on her temple, feeling a headache coming on. "Girl, I know, I know. Please! Just bear with me.

KC's been driving me crazy all morning. She put the cape around Tiffany's neck and leaned her head back into the sink. "Lately he's been gettin' on my fuckin' nerves."

"What? I thought you said KC was all that."

"I didn't say he wasn't." She squirted shampoo into her hand. "He just be trippin' on bullshit. "She changed the subject.

Tiffany looked relaxed as Misty massaged her scalp on the second shampoo. "Me and my man are going to Mobile in a few days."

"Mobile?" Misty said. "What the hell is in Mobile?"

"He got some family down there. One of his cousins, P'Cola supposed to own a barber and beauty shop. Anyway, he's gonna kick it with him since they haven't seen each other in years."

"And what are you supposed to do while they're getting reac- quainted?"

"He's got a girlfriend. We gon' kick it while the dogs run the streets."

Misty wrapped a towel around Tiffany's head. "Well, I hope you have fun."

"I plan on it."

***

Detective Ramos sat in the lobby of the Coroner's Office smoking on his third cigarette in less than thirty minutes. He ignored the "No Smoking" signs posted on the office walls, just like he did at the police station.

The slim blond woman behind the front desk grew tired of repeatedly tellin' him to stop. With a spasm of irritation on her face, she stared at the tall detective as he put the cigarette out in one of the flowerpots.

Dr. Davis, the Medical Examiner, came walking through the double doors, snatching off his surgical mask, to greet the detective.

"Mr. Ramos," the doc said, shaking his hand.

"Doc. What you got for me?"

He took a deep breath. "Well, the victim's name is Javaris Rankin. Twenty-three years of age. I---"

"Spare me the bullshit and give me what I need to build a case. I don't have time for a full analysis."

"Okay, I found pieces of flesh stuck between the victim's front teeth."

"Really?" Detective Ramos said anxiously.

"Yes. We believe it belongs to the killer."

Ramos had his thumb and index finger resting on his chin, thinking. "So what you're saying is there was a tussle and the victim bit the killer?"

"That's exactly what I'm saying," the doctor replied. "Although we won't know for sure until the test results come back from the lab.

Ramos headed for the door. "Get me those results, ASAP," he said over his shoulder. "There's a good chance the suspect has been down before, and we'll already have his DNA on file.

As Ramos left the building, he thought about the story that Misty had told him. She said she saw Javaris attacking the man while she was standing in the doorway watching. There was some truth to what she was saying, so far, he thought. Yet, he still had a gut feeling that she had a connection to the killer.

During a search of what was left of Javaris' burned house, nothing seemed to look out of place. A set up and robbery was what he suspected; however, proving that Misty was involved was another problem.

Ramos hopped inside of his unmarked Crown Victoria, fired up a cigarette, then drove back to headquarters.

***

A week had passed. The Texas sun shone down on KC and Misty's heads while they cruised down Buckner Boulevard in their new convertible Porsche. They wore matching outfits and Cartier sunglasses.

Misty arrogantly turned up her nose at all the pretty girls walking down the streets, half naked, in search of a baller. She felt better than she had in a long time. In less than twenty minutes would be downtown, signing the lease papers for her soon-to-be beauty shop. All of her dreams were becoming reality. She was on top of the world, and nothing could bring her down.

So she thought.

The street light turned red, bringing the Porsche to a halt at the intersection. KC was too busy feeling himself to notice the unmarked police car behind him. Another unmarked car skidded to a stop in front of him as it crossed the intersection. KC and Misty sat stunned as they looked around, realizing that they were being surrounded by police.

Detective Ramos was the first to jump out with his Glock drawn. "Let me see some hands. Now!" he yelled with authority.

"Hands in the air, Miss," a short, young detective yelled, approaching Misty's side of the car.

They put up their hands slowly. Misty's heart was beating so rapidly, she thought it was about to jump out of her chest.

Ramos snatched open the door, immediately pulling KC out by his neck. KC's reflexes caused him to jerk away defensively.

Ramos pointed the gun at his face. "Think about this good, before I bust your ass. Be smart, not a smart ass."

Seeing the seriousness in the detective's eyes, KC backed down, placing his hands on the hood of the car. Detective Ramos searched and relieved him of the chrome Desert Eagle tucked in his pants. Then he escorted him to the police car.

"Out of the car, Miss Thang, the short detective ordered. "Nice and slow."

"What's this all about?" Misty asked as she got out of the car. "We ain't done noth---"

Her voice trailed off when she saw Ramos approaching her.

"Miss Munsey," he said, flashing a superior grin. "Good seeing you again."

"We didn't do anything."

"Sure you didn't." Ramos looked to his short partner. "Cuff her."

Von Diesel

CHAPTER EIGHT

Misty found herself sitting inside the same small room she had been in the day of the robbery. Nervously she sat with her legs trembling. Trying to calm herself down, she had already bitten off three of her manicured fingernails.

Conspiracy to murder was the charge. She wondered how much she could trust KC, not that they had been caught. Would he hold up or would he let her go down for the murder alone?

Finally, Detective Ramos entered the room in a cloud of smoke. Surprisingly, her legs had stopped shaking. She pulled herself together, preparing for whatever questions he had for her to answer.

Ramos spent almost an hour in the room, drilling her with questions about the night of the robbery. But it was useless. She was sticking to the same story that she had already told him. She never saw the face of Javaris' attacker, and if it were KC who killed him, she knew nothing about it.

Frustrated with getting nowhere with her. Ramos jumped up and slammed the steel door behind him as he left the room. He walked down the hall a few feet, then entered another room. KC was slumped down in a chair with a mean look on his face when Ramos walked in.

"I want to talk to my lawyer," KC said to him. Ramos sat on the edge of the table, right next to KC.

"Okay, but first let me ask you this. You know you done fucked up, don't you?" He chuckled. "Aw, man. I've always wanted to say that."

"I ain't did nothin', homie," KC replied confidently.

"Yeah? Well, do you care to explain how pieces of your flesh...got stuck...in between the teeth...of Javaris Rankin?" Ramos asked slowly.

KC looked confused. "Who?"

Ramos yelled, "Javaris Rankin! The man that you robbed and killed." He really wasn't sure about the robbery part. He only said that to see if KC would tell on himself. Ramos shrugged. "Of course, we only think you did it. We'll have it up to a jury to decide if you're really guilty or not. Then maybe we can get something to stick on your girl, too." Ramos took out a Kool and lit it. He took a drag, then slowly blew the smoke into KC's face. "You still need a lawyer?"

KC sat there with a lost look on his face. The bad news struck him like a blow from a sledgehammer. He knew just what Ramos was getting at--either plead guilty to the charge, or we're gonna take your girl down with you. He thought about Misty, and how long it would be before she felt her tender touch again.

Since it was his slip-up that had gotten them caught, he decided to take the weight by himself. He figured that there was no sense in both of them going down for the same crime. Plus, with her on the street, he wouldn't have to worry about money while he was locked down. He had faith in her that she would be down with him until the end.

"Nah, I don't need a lawyer," he replied in a low voice.

"Good." Ramos reached for the tape recorder that sat in the middle of the table. He pushed the record button. "State your full name for the record."

Basically, KC told him the same story that Misty had told them. Only he added that he was the guy who showed up at the door, arguing with Javaris. He admitted to shooting Javaris after being attacked by him. Even though it was Javaris' home, he still had the right to defend himself. He didn't come there to kill him. Things just turned out that way.

Afterward, KC decided that he might as well hit the safe. After Javaris was still breathing, he dragged him down into the basement and forced him to open it. Then, he got a burst of energy from somewhere and tried to attack him again. That's when Javaris bit KC. Two more shots were fired, knocking the life out of him. It would've been foolish to have killed him and not gotten anything out of it.

"Ramos' eyes narrowed on KC. "What were you two arguing about?"

KC took a deep breath. "I found out that Misty was cheating on me with some drug dealer who drove a Hummer. So I chilled out down the street from her aunt's house, saw them together, then followed them to his house. When he answered the door naked, I knew that I interrupted something. I confronted him, things got out of hand and you know the rest."

Ramos thought back to Misty's statement. She had told him that she heard the man at the door asking about some girl. So far, their stories were adding up.

He started pacing the floor." So that's the reason she was able to escape. You never intended to hurt her?"

KC shook his head.

Ramos shut off the recorder. "Malone," he hollered.

A tall, red-haired white man peeked his head into the room, "Yeah?"

Ramos buttoned his navy blue blazer. "Book him, then cut the broad loose," he said evenly. He exited the room without another word.

KC had a wounded look on his face when Malone escorted him out of the room. As they inched down the hallway, KC caught a glimpse of Misty's face through an open door. Ramos was standing over her, probably breaking the bad news. Her face was scarlet red and eyes swollen from crying. KC stopped suddenly., He looked at her as if it would be the last time he saw her. Now he wished that he could be at home, eating her terrible cooking.

"Move!" Malone said harshly. "Pretty girls like that don't wait around for murderers like you to get out the can." He chuckled. "You're looking...at least twenty-five years, punk."

"You must be mad 'cause you won't ever get the chance to bone a pretty girl like mine, cracker." KC said defensively.

Malone frowned. "Get your smart ass down the hall!" He pushed KC in the back. "Let's go."

***

Tears flowed down Misty's face while she sat in the back seat of a cab. Her man was in jail, probably for life, which left her alone. She never knew her mother, and her father was killed by some Crips back before the peace treaty. She had her aunt, but she was too busy chasing the rock to even fool with her own kids, let alone Misty.

Everything happened so fast. One minute they were riding in luxury, about to handle some business. The next, her whole life had been ruined. In the blink of an eye, and without warning, KC had been taken away from her.

The beefy-faced cab driver kept staring at her through his rearview mirror. He wondered if the sad look on her face was because of money troubles. He'd give up his whole take-home for a taste of that vanilla cream. He hurriedly shifted his eyes to the front window when she looked up, catching him staring for the hundredth time.

It was just her luck that she was being stalked by an ugly, perverted cab driver. All she wanted to do was get to KC's house. Then she could pack her things and split with all the money.

Her cell phone rang.

She searched her purse until she found it. "Hello, she said with a crack in her voice.

"Misty, this is Tiffany." She was back in town.

"Hey, girl." She wiped the tears from her eyes.

"The police kicked in KC's house," Tiffany said excitedly. "Girl, they took everything but the kitchen sink. What's going on?"

Misty tried to remain calm while she told Tiffany everything that had gone down. She left out a few details. It wasn't hard for Tiffany to figure out, because she knew what she and KC were into. The cab driver was all ears, trying to hear what was being said. To his disappointment, money wasn't what was troubling her.

"What you gonna do now? Tiffany asked, concerned about her friend. "You can't go back there."

"I don't know, girl," Misty said distantly. "I wish I could get out of town, start all over. Ya know?"

They sat quietly on the phone for what seemed like forever. Tiffany wanted to speak, but had nothing encouraging to say to her friend. They had experienced some rough times together, but Misty was the one who usually knew what to do.

"Ooh, ooh, I know," Tiffany finally said. "Why don't you move to Mobile? You could hook up with Ashton's cousin, P'Cola. He can hook you up with a job at his beauty shop and help you find a place to stay."

"Mobile? Ain't that where Rita and her ol' man is headed to?"

"Yes. They normally go down there once a year for a vacation."

"What about KC? I've got to be there for him. It's because of me that he's in that place."

"No it ain't," Tiffany disagreed. "You said yourself that it was his DNA they found. Plus, he can't do you no good sitting in jail for twenty-five years. It's an ugly thing to say, but it's the truth."

"You're right about that. It sounds good, but how an I supposed to leave town with no money?""

Hearing those last two words caught the cabby's attention. He focused his gaze back into the rearview mirror. This time he didn't avert his eyes when they met with Misty's. He tried hard to suppress an all too incriminating smile.

Misty said, "On second thought, I think I've just found the money for my plane ticket." She flashed the driver a knowing smile.

"Good!" Tiffany exclaimed. "I'll have Ashton call P'Cola and set things up. You can spend the night here, then leave tomorrow."

"See you in a little while," Misty said before hanging up. "Hey sexy."

"Huh?" the driver said nervously. He became aroused by the seductive look in her brown eyes.

"Why don't you pull over somewhere quiet so we can have some fun?" She reached over the seat, rubbing his saggy chest.

65

The cabby happily drove a short distance and turned like it hadn't been used in years. He shut off the engine and looked back at her.

"Come sit back here," she said, patting the seat next to her. She watched him eagerly hop out of the car and run around the front of the car to the back.

She eased her small pocket knife out of her purse, stuffing into her bra. Her mind wasn't made up about how she was going to do it yet. If she made the wrong move, the big man might take her knife and have his way with her.

Sliding in next to her, he removed his hat, revealing a half bald, gray head. He reeked of vodka and cheap cologne. She tried her best not to vomit all over the stinking, pudgy man.

"How much?" he said huskily.

"That depends on what you're trying to do, daddy," she said, imitating one of the whores that she had seen on TV. "How much are you trying to spend?"

"Whatever it takes." Subconsciously he massaged his crotch. "What do you wanna do?"

"Hmm?" What do I want to do? I want my cat licked. Can you do that for me, daddy?"

He flashed a devilish grin. "Sure, I could do that." He put his hand on her thigh.

"Unt unh," she said, removing his liver-spotted hand. "Money first." She stuck out her small hand.

He pulled a roll of money out of his breast pocket. He counted out two hundred dollars, then handed it to her. She didn't care how much he gave her. She was gonna take it all anyway.

"That's for cock, butt and head," he said strongly.

Her eyebrows shot up, Butt and head? Who the fuck does he think I am? she thought. It didn't matter. She would get the money without giving up anything. She watched closely while he stuck the rest of the bills into his sock. Misty lay back against the door. He began slobbering all over her stomach. Savagely, he kissed her while he roughly undid her zipper. Carefully, she eased the knife out of her bra. The clicking sound of the knife being opened caused his beefy face to look up. He shrieked out in pain as the knife came down on his shoulder.

"You crazy bitch!" he screamed. "Gimme that knife" He tried to grab it, only to get stuck again and again.

Misty was careful not to hit a main artery. She had killed once because she had to. It was an experience that she didn't want to go through a second time if she could avoid it.

The pudgy man lay against the back seat, bleeding like a slaughtered hog. She could see him taking slow, deep breaths and knew that he was still alive. She held the knife tight inside her hand while she took the rest of the money out of his sock. He held his wounds while she relieved him of his earnings. The pain was too great to risk being stuck again.

Misty climbed into the front seat. After ripping the wires out of the CB radio, she took his car keys and ran off. Once she was out of his sight, she stopped beside an oak tree. Tired and gasping for air, she called Tiffany on her cell phone to pick her up.

***

The next day, Tiffany and Misty stood outside of the airport, embracing one another. They had been up all night talking about the past, when times were better. They were friends to the end, but it was time for Misty to move on. Although Dallas was a big city, Tiffany also thought it was a good idea for Misty to get away. She had either done, or been involved in, too many robberies of too many different people.

Misty grabbed her bag and left to board her plane. Tiffany waved goodbye, wishing her friend a safe journey. She wasn't worried about her surviving. If anybody could start a new life in a strange place, with only a couple of hundred dollars to start with, it was Misty. She was smart, tough and could handle her own.

After a bumpy plane ride to Mobile Regional Airport, Misty thanked God that she made it safely. Inside the airport, she found the bar where she was told that P'Cola would meet her. It was nearly empty. She took a seat at the bar and ordered a Crown and Coke, while she waited for P'Cola to show.

Stacy, P'Cola's girlfriend, stood in the doorway, eyeing the dimly lit bar. She scoped the room until she came across a doll-faced woman sitting all alone at the end of the bar. She could tell by the lonely look on her face that she was the woman she had been sent to get. Stay strutted her slim frame over to where Misty was sitting.

"You Misty?" Stacy asked smartly. Now that she was up close, she could see that Misty's face had a fading bruise on the side. other than that, there wasn't a blemish or a mark on it, and she wasn't even wearing makeup. Instantly, Stacy became jealous, knowing that P'Cola would find her very attractive.

"Yes," she answered defensively. She could tell by the evil glare in Stacy's eyes that she didn't like what she saw.

"My man, P'Cola, told me to come pick you up." Stacey made damn sure she knew that P'Cola was her man.

They got into Stacy's Chrysler 300. She put on her yellow-framed Gucci glasses. She gave Misty a quick glance to see if she was impressed.

She wasn't.

"There's no smoking, eating or drinking in my car." Stacy informed her. She had no idea what type of woman she was dealing with.

"I don't smoke," Misty replied. She faced Stacy. "Let's get something straight, right now, bitch." Stacy's mouth fell open. "You ain't got no reason to be mean to me. I don't want your man or nothing else you have. Now if there's another problem, we can get out and handle it right now."

Stacy's eyes widened with alarm. She sat there in stunned silence, not knowing what to say. Without a word, she put her car into drive and pulled away.

***

P'Cola stepped his blubbery body out of the tub, drying off with a green Polo towel. Admiring himself in the mirror, he applied cocoa butter to the dark area where his beard hairs had been cut. He couldn't wait until Stacy showed up with their new house guest. If she was as fine as Tiffany said she was, he was definitely gonna hit it.

The house looked empty when the two women walked into the living room. Avante was playing softly out of the stereo, and they could smell incense burning. Stacy dropped her purse and keys on the table on her way out to the patio to look for P'Cola.

Misty stopped her. "Which way is the bathroom?"

Stacy pointed a freshly manicured nail. "Down the hall, first door on the right."

Assuming it was unoccupied, Misty walked into the bathroom without knocking. To her surprise, P'Cola was standing in front of the sink, naked. She couldn't help but look down to catch a glimpse of what he was working with.

"Who you?" P'Cola asked, unashamed of being naked in front of her.

Misty flinched, covering her mouth with her hand. "I'm sorry. I didn't meant to--"

"Don't trip on it. You must be Misty."

"Yes." She started to back away. "Excuse me."

"Nah. Excuse me." He stepped around her. Go ahead. My house is your house.

Misty stepped inside, closing the door behind her. She took a deep breath and shook her head. She couldn't believe what just happened. She hadn't been there for five minutes and had already seen him naked. If Stacy got wind of that, they would be fighting for real.

She pulled down her pants and sat on the toilet. Soon after, she heard P'Cola and Stacy arguing. She leaned closer to the door trying to hear what was being said.

"I thought I did, too," P'Cola said, lying as usual. "But Bip changed his mind."

"So, what you're telling me is that tramp has to live under my roof until God knows when? I don't think so," Stacy snapped. Her eyes narrowed on P'Cola suspiciously. "Wait a minute. I know you, P'Cola. You done that shit on purpose. Didn't you?"

"I didn't do shi--"

"Yes you did, nigga. Your fat ass think you're slick. Let me catch you in the bed with that ho and I'm gonna stab the shit outta both of y'all's asses."

P'Cola closed the bedroom door so Misty couldn't hear them talking about her.

Misty stared at her reflection in the mirror while she washed her hands. "Girl, what have you gotten yourself into?"

CHAPTER NINE

The annoying sound of Roseshell's cell phone ringing woke Keith. He rolled to the left, then to the right, trying to get comfortable. He looked over at Roseshell who was sleeping peacefully. He shook his head. He was about to get up and answer it himself, but it stopped ringing.

Getting up out of the bed, he threw his hands up, stretching his long chiseled frame. After doing a hundred push-ups and crunches, he jumped into the shower. He started singing. "We belong together, hmmm. And you knoooow that I'm right. How could you love me and leave me and never...say goodbye." He loved that song by Boyz II Men.

Roseshell woke up to the sound of Keith's lovely singing voice. Even though he skipped parts of the song, it still sounded good. Her long sorrel-colored hair hung down over her face. It went well with her cream skin tone. His singing was beginning to make her moist between the legs.

She had come over drunk last night, expecting to get fucked real good. Her plans were spoiled when Keith said that he was too tired from working all day. She knew the truth. What he really meant was that he was too tired from fucking one of his younger bitches.

What is it gonna take to hook this young nigga? Roseshell wondered. She fucked him good, bought him things and paid his car note. What else can I do?

She removed the covers from her body after she heard the shower cut off. She lay on her back, spread eagle, waiting on him to come out of the bathroom. She could see her nipples swelling in front of her eyes. Her hormones were on fire.

The bathroom door opened. Keith appeared in the doorway, toweling himself dry. "Goddamn!" he exclaimed, seeing her lying naked across his bed. Her almond-shaped hazel eyes watched him seductively. Slowly, her eyelids shut and she bit down on her bottom lip, pretending that he was deep inside of her. She rubbed her clit and jammed three fingers in and out of herself. She stared at her sex nest that matched the hair on her head, probably inherited from her mother, who was Dutch.

Keith picked up his watch off the dresser. It was seven thirty in the morning, and he had to be at work by eight. He cleared his throat to get her attention.

"Huh?" she said in a strangled voice. She had almost reached her climax.

He pointed to the sign over his door. Check out time is seven thirty a.m., she read to herself. "That sign ain't for me. That's for them other hoes that you be creeping around with. I hope you use protection."

"Roseshell, that sign is for anyone who doesn't live here," he corrected her. "Now get your thick ass up. I've got to get ready for work."

Her cell phone started ringing again. She got up, stomping her long, busty body over to the dresser. Keith couldn't help but check out her big, jiggly ass as she stepped. She caught him staring and rolled her eyes at him.

"Hello," she said into the phone. "Oh, hey, Jermaine baby." She looked at Keith, putting her index finger up to her lips, signaling him to be quiet.

How the fuck can she make me be quiet in my own house? he thought. Bitch has got a lot of nerve.

"Un huh," she said. "You're at the barbershop getting your haircut? Okay. I'll be home in a few. You know I was at work last night. Come on Jermaine, don't start." She sighed and put her hand on her forehead. She was tired of Jermaine's bitching. "Well, you should've called me at work if you didn't believe me. By, Jermaine." She pushed the end button, disconnecting him.

By the time she got off the phone, Keith was already dressed. He had on a pair of Ralph Loren slacks, a Polo shirt and tie and black square-toed dress shoes. She watched lustfully, as he brushed his wavy hair and goatee. He was thinking that he should've been a model for GQ magazine. Unknown to him, Roseshell was thinking the exact same thing.

In the dresser mirror, he noticed that Roseshell had gotten back into his bed. She looked so sexy sitting up naked and mad, but she had to obey the rules just like all the others.

"Roseshell, it's seven forty," he said harshly.

"And? What's that supposed to mean?"

He nodded his head toward the check-out sign.

"I ain't no ho," she snapped. "How are you just gonna kick me out? You know what? Fuck it!" She began putting on her clothes.

He watched her pull her pink panties over her backside.

"I come over here expecting to make love and end up playing with myself. You ain't all that. I could've stayed at home with the old man if I wanted to get finger fucked. Shit!" she pouted.

She finished dressing, grabbed her purse, and headed to the door. On her way out, she stopped to glance at her watch. "Seven-forty-four. You happy?"

"Roseshell, don't act like that, baby," he said, trying to comfort her. "You knew the rules when you came over last night."

"You're right," she agreed. "Since I have to obey them, you don't have to worry about my fine ass lying in your bed no more." She left, slamming the door behind her.

"Good, you lazy-ass bitch," he said to himself. He smirked as he looked out his front window and watched her bolt down the street in her Land Rover.

Had he looked to his right, he would've seen her husband parked down the street, sitting low in his BMW. He waited until he saw Keith's curtain closer before he pulled off.

***

The dealership was filled with customers when Keith pulled up and parked in his reserved parking spot. He spotted Devontae showing a tall, big-boned girl a new Nissan Maxima. The cool look on his face made it seem more like he was macking than trying to sell a car. Keith strolled past them into the building. While he was unlocking his office door, he saw Jason out of the corner of his eye. "Hey, my favorite white boy," Keith said jokingly. "What's up with ya?"

"Chillin'," he replied, trying to sound black. "I need to talk to you for a minute, homie."

"A'ight." Keith led Jason into his office. He flipped on the lights. "Have a seat." He made himself comfortable in the high-black leather chair behind his desk. "Talk to me."

Jason took a deep breath. "Man, yo, like I got this big problem with gettin' girls. Right? And since I know you're a player, I was hoping that you could give some pointers, or somethin' like that." Jason looked at him through serious eyes.

Keith was aware that Jason thought of himself as black. He didn't like it, but he dealt with it because he knew that Jason was a good dude. Plus, Jason looked up to him. Every time he had a problem, he would go to Keith for answers instead of his father, Mr. Morris, who was the owner of Down the Bay Ford dealership.

"What kinda game can I give a white boy, Jason? I don't have one white broad in my stable of whores, man."

Jason jumped to his feet. "Man, cut the bullshit, Keith, man," he snapped. "I know what be going on up in this office. I ain't no damn fool. I hear the girls that come in here making moaning sounds and shit. You a stud, man. That's why I came to you."

An incriminating smile flashed across Keith's face. "First off, Jason, with you being white, you could never possess the game that I have. So don't think that you're ever gonna be on my level, no matter how much I teach you," Keith said arrogantly.

"I'm not trying to compete with you," he explained. "All I need you to do is gimme some game that'll make me feel more confident about myself."

Jason searched his pockets. He placed a wad of crumpled bills on top of Keith's desk, then counted them. "I've got two hundred and ten, no, eleven dollars."

"Give me the two hundred." Keith leaned forward, snatching it out of his hand. Jason watched him stuff the money into his pocket. "Now, here's what I want you to do. Change your dress code. Go with the casual look instead of the wannabe Eminem look. You ain't no damn rapper. Imagine how silly I would look if I walked around dressed like Andre 3000 from Out Kast. You think my woman would respect me dressed like that?"

"Nah," Jason replied, feeling what he was saying.

Keith pressed on. "Next, you've got to be aggressive with a woman. Talk to her with authority. Tell me what you say when you walk up to a woman that you're attracted to? Pretend that she's a black girl."

Jason thought for a moment. "A'ight. I'll walk up to her and say, "Didn't I see you in a Jay-Z video?" He smiled, thinking he had said something fly. He frowned after seeing the unimpressed look on Keith's face. "What's wrong with that?"

Keith sighed. "That's the lamest shit I've ever heard in my life. Any real broad would've slapped the shit out of your ass."

Jason looked dumbfounded. Keith stood up and walked over to his file cabinet. He searched through the files until he found the one he was looking for. "Let me show you how this shit's done, boy."

"What you doing?" Jason quizzed.

Keith sat back down in his chair. "Remember that little green-eyed girl that I sold the Mustang to a few weeks ago?"

"The one that was in here moaning?" Jason said.

"Yeah, smart ass," Keith replied. He punched her number into the office phone, then turned on the speaker. "Take notes."

Jason made himself comfortable in order to watch the mack in action. Her phone rang twice before she picked up. "I sent your check, K'Mo," she said, answering the phone. Obviously she had seen the number come up on the caller ID.

Keith looked cautiously at Jason to see if he was paying attention to what she had said. The last thing he wanted was for the cover to be blown off his scam. Jason didn't flinch; he was too busy waiting on Keith to put his mack down.

"I ain't on that right now," Keith said smoothly. "I called to see how you were doing." He leaned back in his chair.

"Really?" she said. "I'm sorry. I thought this was a business call."

"Unt unh. So, how's your car holding up?"

"It's cool, I'm happy. I get a lot of attention in it. Especially when I've got the top down," she bragged.

"That's good. I love a satisfied customer. Look, Kylie. I've been thinking about you ever since that day. I finally built up the nerve to call you."

"Yeah, right," she said doubtfully. "Since when did you start having to build up the nerve to talk to a woman? You know, I heard about you long before I met you."

Keith shifted in his seat. "See, that's the thing. Something's different about you. I don't know what it is, but I get a queasy feeling in my stomach just by talking to you."

She laughed softly. "Boy, you are something else. So tell me, to what do I owe the pleasure of you calling lil' ole me?"

"Umm...how about you buying me dinner?" He winked his eye at Jason. "Is this Sunday cool?"

"Yeah, that's cool," she agreed. "What time?"

"Probably around eight. Call me. You got my number."

"I sure will. Bye, sexy."

He hung up. "That's how easy it is, he explained. "I came at her like she was all that. Then she came back at me with the same game." He pointed his long finger at him. "That right there gave me the go ahead to be aggressive with her. You see how I told her what she was gonna do? Even after I taxed her for that bullshit-ass car, she's still gonna take me out to dinner." He shrugged. "It's as simple as that."

Jason looked at Keith like he was his savior. He stood up. "Damn, bro. You a cold piece, man. I'ma do it exactly like you did, since it's that easy." Jason walked to the door. He stopped suddenly, turning around. "What about my money?" he asked curiously.

A dirty grin appeared on Keith's face. "Like I said before, the game is to be sold, not told."

Finally, Jason got the message. He left, closing the door behind him.

Keith called Fabien on the phone. It rang for what seemed like forever before he answered.

"Hello."

"Meet me for lunch 'round," he glanced at his watch, "twelve o'clock. I gotta holla at you about something."

"That's cool. Let's go to The Boiling Pot on Airport this time. I'm tired of WingStop," Fabien complained.

"It don't make no difference to me. See you in a few," Keith hung up.

Stepping around his huge desk, he walked over to the big window that overlooked the many rows of new cars. Devontae was leading an attractive but healthy female customer inside. He smiled, knowing that Devontae was probably gonna offer her a loan from his personal bank. He could just imagine what she would look like bent over Devontae's small desk.

Von Diesel

78

CHAPTER TEN

The mid-afternoon traffic was heavy when Keith hopped onto the freeway. The Camaro's big engine roared as he weaved through the traffic. Devontae sat on the passenger side, holding on for his life. He wanted to say something, but he knew it wouldn't do any good. Keith turned into another person when he was behind the wheel.

Their exit was coming up. He quickly whipped the Camaro to the right, barely missing the back end of a Honda Accord. He didn't bother slowing down as he got onto the Government Boulevard Exit. Ignoring the red light, he made a left, spinning his tires like he was racing.

Devontae had enough. "Man slow this muh-fucker down," he hollered. "Kill yo'self, but don't take me with you."

Keith slowed down. Man, I swear you act like a bitch sometimes. I'ma start callin' you little bitch instead of little Devontae." Keith shook his head in disgust. "Get behind the wheel of the muthafucka and you'll see why I drive like this."

"Mmm hm. You gon' see too after you end up wrapped around a damn pole."

Keith laughed, easing to a stop at a red light. It felt good to be a young player. The summer was approaching and he couldn't wait to see what new bitches would be coming out of hibernation this year.

He faced Devontae. "Man, did you---" Something caught his attention.

The baddest bitch that he had ever seen pulled up next to him in a black Excursion. He could hear Beyonce and Jay-Z's "Upgrade You" belting out of it. She was in her own little world as she sang along, bobbing her head to the beat.

She sang", Let me, let me upgrade you." Her long, silky mane blew in the wind.

Even from a distance, he could see her shiny, olive-colored skin. She must have felt him watching her, because she turned her head and looked in his direction.

Her mouth fell open when she saw Keith's face. Damn, that nigga looks just like KC, she thought. It was kind of scary looking at him, knowing that KC was all the way in Dallas, locked up. She took off her dark shades, revealing her slanted eyes. They exchanged predatory looks.

Devontae noticed the look on Keith's face. He turned, following Keith's eyes, to see what had his attention. Devontae's face took on the same look after he saw her.

"Man, what you waiting on?" he said, nudging Keith. "You better get on that." He knew that she was out of his league.

When the light turned green, Misty winked at him salaciously, then pulled off. He felt a dark cloud over his head after he saw her license plates. They read: PCOLA.

"Ain't that P'Cola's truck?" Devontae said.

Keith sat with a gloomy look on his face. He could tell by her eyes that she had game for a nigga. She was exactly the type he was looking for. Out of all the dudes in Mobile who were eligible, P'Cola had gotten her first.

People cursing and blowing their horns behind him brought him back to reality. He was about to drive off, but the light had turned red again. "Move, Goddamn it! Are you color blind?" Get some fuckin' glasses!" he heard people yelling from their cars.

"I reminded her of somebody," Keith said to no one in particular. "She thought she recognized me from somewhere."

Devontae looked at his watch. "You'd better recognize and hurry the fuck up. We gotta be back at the office at one."

The light turned green again. Keith pulled off. "Shut the fuck up, nigga."

"Aw, you tough now, right." Devontae laughed. "Nigga, you been exposed."

Keith looked confused. "What are you talking about?"

"You been scared to holla at that bitch. I just wanna put that on record." Devontae laughed. "First time I ever saw you freeze up."

Keith bit down on his bottom lip, kind of embarrassed by Devontae's comment. He had to admit, the sight of Misty did stun

80

him for a moment, though he would never admit it out loud. "Laugh now," Keith said. "I guess I'ma have to get at her just to show you that she ain't no different than the rest." He said that to save face. "I treat bad bitches like shit, too."

"A'ight, Too Short."

"Watch and see, sucka. I'ma make that ho bust her feet and her wallet," he said with confidence. "P'Cola gon' have to be mad at me.

The Boiling Pot was crowded with working people from various on their lunch breaks. Waiters and waitresses bumped back and forth, trying to satisfy the impatient customers. Today's special was the Shrimp Platter. Devontae and Keith entered the dimly lit place, scanning the room for Fabien. They had seen his Black Escalade parked out front.

They spotted his wavy, peanut head sitting at a booth near the back. Devontae pointed in his direction. Fabien had a big grin on his face while he talked into his cell phone. He glanced up at the two sitting down at the table.

"I'll see you on Friday," Fabien said into the phone. "You too, Bye." He hung up. He looked back and forth between the two, who were looking at him accusingly. "What?"

"You trick-ass nigga, Devontae said jokingly. "We know what 'you too' means."

"Yeah," Keith said. "You should've just said, 'I love you too'."

"Fuck both of you niggas," Fabien said defensively. He folded up his menu. "I already ordered three samplers."

"Works for me," Keith agreed, along with Devontae.

The waitress brought over three oval-shaped places full of chicken, pork, beef and three side dishes. Quietly, they all sat scarfing down the delicious combination of food.

While they were eating, Keith noticed a very attractive young black woman dining alone across the room. He kept staring at her, hoping to get her attention. His heart almost leaped out of his chest when he saw a man that he knew too well come out of nowhere and join her at the table. It was James.

"Keith had always suspected James of cheating on his mama, but actually seeing it was something different. He decided to keep it to himself for the time being. He didn't intend to bring chaos to his mother's home, but he would check James about it later.

"Man, what you over there daydreaming about?" Fabien asked, bringing him back to reality.

"Yeah, nigga. Where the fuck yo' mind at?" Devontae asked.

Keith wiped his mouth with a paper napkin. "I was thinking about something," he lied. "Devontae, what the hell did you do with that fat-ass girl that I saw you taking to your office?"

"Aw, man." Devontae paused to wipe his mouth. "I fucked the shit out of her big pretty ass. Pussy was wet as a muthafucka. I made her pay a big down payment. After wrestling with her big-ass thighs, I thought I deserved a little extra."

"You niggas is silly," Fabien stated. "Y'all gon' fuck around and get fired and put up under the jail."

Devontae took a sip of his Coke. "Man, we're doing them bitches a favor. Ain't nobody gonna tell. You should see how eager those girls be to give it up. They want them new cars as bad as fiends want crack. The fucked up thing is, they think they're getting over."

Keith nodded his head in agreement. "I didn't think it would work out this well, either. But it does. I can remember when a bitch would come in qualified for a ten thousand dollar loan, but wanted a twelve thousand dollar car and didn't have a dime in her pocket. Eventually, we'd end up knocking off two grand to fit her budget. That's why the cars are all over-priced anyway. So we started charging extra, then told the boss that we knocked it off the price. And I must say, my bank account has been looking pretty good ever since."

"Fabien said," Don't call me to bail y'all asses out, and don't write me from county, because I ain't gon' be coming up to visit you niggas." He paused. "Now what was it that you wanted to talk to me about? I gotta be somewhere in a minute."

"Aw, yeah," Keith said. He glanced around the room to see if anybody was listening before he whispered, "I need you to get me a gun."

Fabien sat back and sucked his teeth while he pondered the request. Actually, he knew where to get one, he just wasn't sure if he should tell Keith or not. Keith was a player who didn't know much about the street life except how to chase hoes. If Keith fucked around and did something stupid with it, it would be on his conscience.

"What a nigga like you need a gun for?" Fabien quizzed.

"Because. You never know when one of them ole hating-ass niggas is gonna want to trip over some broad," Keith explained.

"If one of 'em finds out that they girl is paying my bills, ain't no telling what they might try." He paused, realizing what Fabien said. "What you mean? What a nigga like me need with a gun? You saying I'm a bitch or something?"

Fabien put his hand up. "Hold on, Keith. I know you ain't no bitch. I was just saying. How many niggas that wear Armani suits walk around carrying guns?" Fabien's voice softened. "That ain't your style. That's all I'm saying."

"I can see where ya coming from," Keith said. "But I still want one."

Fabien took a deep breath. "Aight. Let's go outside." He wiped his mouth and threw the napkin on his plate. Keith picked up the tab, then followed Fabien out to his truck. He reached into his glove compartment and pulled out a brand new Glock. He wiped his prints off with the sleeve of his shirt and handed it to Keith.

"You can have this," Fabien offered. "If you have to use it, get rid of it."

Keith held the gun like it was a newborn baby. He aimed it at a parked car. "I like this."

"Fabien got into his truck. "Just remember what I said."

Keith and Devontae got back inside the Camaro. He tucked it away inside the console then cautiously headed back to work.

***

This time it wasn't the garage door window that was broken when he got home. It was the living room window. Pissed off, Keith hopped out, hit the alarm, and flew into the house. He picked up the phone, dialing Natalie's number.

"Hello," she answered, trying to sound innocent.

"Bitch! I know it was you who busted out my damn window. You're gonna keep fuckin' with me and I'ma end up poppin' the shit out of yo' ass."

"With what?" She laughed. "Nigga, you don't even own a gun."

"You gon' find out with what, bitch," he retorted. "Keep on fuckin' with my shit."

"Is that how you talk to me?" Her voice was serious now. "I help pay bills around that muthafucka and I don't even get to spend the night." Her voice cracked as she began to cry. "The least you could do is drop by and say hi or something. Act like you care about me a little bit, damn."

He fixed himself a glass of cognac, while she sniffled in his ear. The silence would settle her down.

She sniffled again. "Hello?"

"I'm here. I'm just letting you get it all off your chest."

"I've said all I have to say."

He took a sip of his drink. "I know I have been neglecting you lately." His voice was calm. "I promise I'ma make all of this up to you." Keith walked over to the fireplace and began going through yesterday's mail.

"See how easy that was? I know I be overreacting. I just want some attention. And don't worry, I'm going to get your window fixed."

"You didn't have to tell me that."

"When am I gonna see you?"

"Tonight. I'm feeling a little tense and in need of one of your massages. Bring the baby oil."

"Cool. I'm gonna pick up some motion lotion on my way over there. It heats up when you blow on it."

"Natalie."

"Yes, baby?"

"You don't have any boyfriends that I should know about, do you?" he asked curiously.

"Naw, boy. You know that I'm too in love with your scandalous ass to fuck around with anybody else. I ain't nasty like that."

"I was just askin'. I'll see you in a minute." He hung up.

He opened the mail he received from his loan customers and placed the checks inside his wallet. He smiled when he saw the money order with Kylie's name on it.

After taking Roseshell's portrait down, he replaced it with Natalie's. Then he jumped into the shower to freshen up. Since Natalie didn't have a man, the gun would remain in the car for tonight.

Like a pimp, he wasn't too fond of fucking his broads on a regular basis. That made them lose focus and could cause tender dick---a serious disease that made a man develop feelings for a broad. But Natalie was long overdue for a good fucking. Tonight he would give her enough dick to satisfy her for a month.

Von Diesel

CHAPTER ELEVEN

Things were beginning to look up for Misty, P'Cola had given her a booth at the beauty shop and secretly bought her a whole new wardrobe. She also got to drive his truck until she could save enough money to buy her own car.

Supposedly, P'Cola was still trying to find her a place to stay, but he hadn't found anything. Too bad, because she couldn't stand living under the same roof as Stacy.

Already they had gotten into two catfights and had countless arguments with each other. Stacy did everything she could to annoy Misty. Especially when she and P'Cola had sex. Stacy would moan and scream at the top of her lungs, just to try to make Misty jealous. What she didn't know was that she was doing just the opposite. She made Misty wonder how the big man would feel between her thighs, humping her like a savage beast. She already knew that he was a potential risk. But since P'Cola was Tiffany's man's cousin, she decided to try to keep from breaking up their happy home. She'd use them to help her get back on her feet, then bounce.

To Stacy's satisfaction, Misty had befriended a girl who had just started working at P'Cola's shop also. Kylie and Misty hung out every day after work. By the time Misty got home, she was too tired to do anything except take a shower and go to bed.

Misty hadn't had sex in nearly a month, and her pussy was on fire. Those late night rubs in the shower weren't cutting it. She needed some sex, and bad. Even if she had to get it from the cute dyke girl they call Star, up at the shop. She hadn't been with another woman before, but she was horny enough to fuck a mule.

Misty took the wrap from around her freshly done head. It was eight, and she had to be at work within the next thirty minutes. Kylie had called ten minutes ago saying that she was on her way.

After she finished taking care of her hygiene, she squeezed into a pair of tight blue jeans, a T-shirt and a pair of black Nikes. She wanted to be comfortable standing on her feet all day. She reminded herself to stop by the mall after work so she could pick up something skimpy to walk around the house in. That would really set Stacy on fire. Misty often wondered why she was so devious.

She was standing in the bathroom mirror applying eye shadow when the doorbell rang. "P'Cola! she yelled. "Could you open up the front door for Kylie, please?"

"Open it yourself," Stacy replied for him.

Misty smiled devilishly. She checked her face in the mirror one last time before she went to get the door.

Kylie was standing there, looking hazel-eyed and fine in a pair of tight stretch pants and a T-shirt. She was very pretty and had a nice shape, but was of no competition to Misty. On a regular day, Misty's doll face looked as if she had been to Glamour Shots for a photo shoot. She could've easily had a career as a top model with her tall and curvy frame. Her ass was fat, but her waist was as small as a twelve-year-old's.

"Kylie stepped her short, thick frame into the living room. "Girl, you ready?"

"Yep. Let me grab my purse." Misty ran down the hall to her bedroom.

***

On their way to work, Kylie decided to tell Misty about her new friend, Keith. "Girl, I met somebody." Kylie said excitedly.

Misty knew that she had detected a new glow in Kylie's hazel eyes. "Really? Is he fine?"

"Fine ain't the word, girl. His face belongs on TV."

"I ain't mad at you. I'll be glad when I find me somebody."

"You and me both." She chuckled. "Girl, yo' pussy is so hot, I can feel steam coming out from between your legs." They shared a laugh. Kylie pulled over to drop her top. "Ooh, that reminds me, girl."

"What?" Misty quizzed.

"He sells cars. He can probably help you get one." Kylie had temporarily forgotten about Keith's loan program, and the possibility of Misty ending up bent over his desk.

"Talk to him and see what he says."

"I will."

"*Let It Go*," by Keyshia Cole, came on the radio. Kylie turned it up. She and Misty sang along all the way to the shop.

***

Kendrick Lamar was performing live on "The Ellen De-Generes Show," and Misty stood in front of the TV, shaking her ass to the music. Nobody but the girls complained about her blocking the forty-inch TV. To the guys in the barbershop, watching her dance was more exciting than watching Kendrick Lamar perform his latest single.

Kylie was putting a relaxer on an older woman's hair and trying to see Kendrick Lamar at the same time. "Girl, yo' daddy wasn't no glass maker," Kylie said to Misty. "Get yo' big butt out from in front of the TV. We trying to see Kendrick Lamar."

"Speak for yourself, girl," Kathea, one of the other beauticians said. "I'm trying to see "Madear.""

Star was finishing up on a young kid's plain haircut. "Do your thang, Misty," she encouraged her. "Matter of fact, you come over here and shake that thang in front of me and Lil' Ant."

Everybody on the barber's side cheered, while the women in the beauty shop all looked at each other. "Unt unh."

Misty spun around, narrowing her pretty browns on Star. "Yours ain't big enough to handle this." She grabbed her crotch.

Junebug's paper fell out of his hand. "Laws have mercy. It's gettin' hot in here."

Misty looked down at him. "What you babbling about, Junebug? If I gave you a whiff of this, you'd probably cum in your pants."

"I don't have a problem with that," he said, matter-of-factly.

A ten-year-old sat in P'Cola's chair, getting his braided hair lined up. "I like coming up in here, P'Cola. Where did you get her from?" he asked, referring to Misty.

P'Cola popped him on the ear. "Shut up and cover your ears. Ay, y'all hold that filth down. We got kids up in here."

"I ain't no kid," the boy said angrily. "I'm almost eleven."

"Eleven," P'Cola repeated. "Boy, your little dick ain't even big enough to hold while you pee."

The boy became embarrassed when he saw everybody including Misty, laughing at him. P'Cola is always showing out, he thought. He sat with his lips stuck out for the rest of the time that he was in the chair.

Misty strutted back over to her booth to her waiting customer to finish twisting his dreadlocks. The light-skinned man was sitting in the chair, waiting patiently. "Girl, you off the chain," he said, flashing his gold-toothed smile. "Round here gettin' everybody aroused and shit."

"Shut up, Blue," she said, hitting him on his shoulder. "I'm just having fun."

P'Cola dusted the hair off of the little boy's neck and helped him down off the booster seat. P'Cola dug into his pocket, pulled out some change, and handed it to the boy.

"Here. Buy you a bag of chips and a soda. Sit down over there until your mother gets back." He pointed to a chair that sat in front of the TV that had the Playstation 4 connected to it. Though his lips were still poked out and he was angry, he did as he was told.

Blue wet his lips, watching Misty's breasts dangle in front of him while he twisted his hair. He never even thought about getting his hair locked up until Misty told him that he had the face for it. She said that they would bring out the color of his eyes. From then on, he stopped letting her braid his hair and switched to dreads.

Blue had been building up the nerve to ask her out for two weeks. He finally decided to go for it. "So, umm...who you fuckin' with? I don't ever hear you talking about a man or nothing."

"If you're trying to ask me out," she looked him in the eye, "don't beat around the bush. Just be a man and come on out with it. All I can say is no." She paused. "Or yes."

"Aight then," he said, building confidence. "Can I take you out?"

"Mmmm, no," she replied. "I don't go out with dudes unless I plan on fuckin' 'em. And I don't fuck my clients." She continued to twist his locks.

He stroked his bearded chin, making an imploring smile. "I can't be an exception?"

She finished the last lock, then took the cape from around his neck. "I would make an exception," she smiled, "but I don't like dudes who wear dreads. Pay up at the counter." She walked away to the restroom, leaving him dumbfounded.

"Dirty bitch," he said to himself.

Junebug laughed. "She's a beast, ain't she?"

Star saw Misty heading toward the back. It was time for her to make her move. She stopped sweeping so she could catch up behind her. Startled, she turned around quickly, thinking that Blue had come after her. To her surprise, Star was standing there with a naughty grin on her face. She nodded her head toward the restroom, inviting Misty inside.

Misty stepped back, putting some distance between them. "What do you want?"

"You know what I want." She reached for Misty's hair. "I want to show you how much of a man I can be."

Misty pushed her hand away. "I don't get down like that."

"Come on, girl," Star pleaded. "You might not have got down like that before, but you will." Star stepped closer to her. Her light brown eyes met Misty's. "Just as i thought, you got a look in your eye like you haven't been fucked in a while." She sniffled. "I can smell the backed-up cum through your jeans."

Star was attractive to Misty. Up close, she looked like a pretty-ass boy. Of course, that could've been Misty's hormones talking. Star licked her lips, focusing her attention on Misty's crotch. Misty could feel the moisture in her panties.

They exchanged scorching looks. All of a sudden, Misty found herself inching into the restroom. By the time Star had locked the door, Misty already had her pants off. They attacked each other, kissing wildly in the middle of the floor. Misty panted and mounted softly while Star skillfully kissed her ears and neck. She stuck her fingers inside of Misty's mouth to muffle the moaning sounds.

"Mmm. Do something to make me um," Misty begged. She removed her panties, hopped up on the sink and gaped her legs wide so Star could go down on her.

Star turned her ball cap to the back and squatted down between her legs. Starting out slow, she slid her tongue into her crevice, wiggling it around inside of her. Misty let out a high pitched howl, then quickly caught herself. While Star expertly nibbled and sucked on her clitoris, she worked two fingers in and out of her. Misty grabbed the back of Star's head, encouraging her to go on.

Star sucked harder when she felt Misty's legs begin to tremble. Misty held her breath when she felt herself cumming. "Here it...comes," she grunted.

"Mm hmm," Star moaned, sucking all of the cum juice out of her. When she finished, she gave it one last kiss before she stood up.

Misty fell back against the mirror with her eyes closed, breathing rapidly. After her breathing slowed, she opened her eyes. Now that she had an orgasm, the thrill was gone. Realizing that it was another woman standing in front of her, she got down and put her panties back on. Star no longer looked like a pretty-ass boy to her. She was a woman, standing there with pussy juice drying around her mouth. Without a word, she put her clothes back on, fixed herself in the mirror, then left Star standing in the restroom. Alone.

P'Cola flipped the channel to BET and had the volume up loud. Misty could hear Meek Mills rapping as she crept over to her booth.

Kylie looked up from styling the older lady's hair. She looked at Misty curiously, noticing the odd look on her face. Being nosey, she glanced down the hall just in time to catch Star leaving the restroom with a sneaky grin on her face.

"Awww," Kylie said, nodding her head in Star's direction," and her doing in the restroom for all that time?

Misty whispered in her ear, "I let her suck my pussy.

Kylie's eyes almost popped out of their sockets. "Girl, are you crazy?"

Misty hit her for talking too loud. "Girl, keep your damn voice down." She took Kylie by the arm, leading her to the back room. "Girl, I needed to bust a nut, bad," she explained. "I was about to explode." She paused while Deryka, the nail technician, walked past them to the restroom. "So what it had to be with a girl," she continued. "It aint never gonna happen again."

"I hope not, because that bitch is trifling."

"Trifling? You've only known her for two weeks, Kylie."

"And?" Kylie said smartly. "I've seen her around. And I've gathered enough to know that she'll fuck anybody who opens their legs."

Misty sighed. "Well, whatever. Just keep this between us. P'Cola would probably kick me out the house if he found out."

"Misty, Kylie," they heard Junebug yell. "I'm about to order some fish. Y'all want some?"

"Yes, please." Kylie replied. "Don't forget that I like extra hot sauce on mine." Kylie turned back to Misty. "I ain't gonna say nothing. Just don't do it again. Please."

"Cross my heart and hope to die," Misty said, making a cross on her heart with her index finger.

Von Diesel

CHAPTER 12

KC's legs shook nervously and his stomach was in knots as he sat beside his lawyer, waiting on the judge to enter the courtroom. Thanks to his public defender, he got the prosecutor to reduce the charge from second degree murder to manslaughter. He kept glancing toward the back of the courtroom, hoping that Misty would walk through the door and take a seat. After all they had been through together, showing up for his sentencing would be the least she could do. After all, if it weren't for him, she would be sitting there, too.

The old, heavyset bailiff stood up. "All rise. This court is now in session. The honorable Judge Charity Holloway presiding."

Everyone in the courtroom stood until they were asked to be seated. Holloway put a pair of half-moon reading glasses onto her grumpy-looking face. Her stony expression scared KC to death. He wished that God would work his magic and get him out of this. If he did, Misty would have hers coming.

The judge kept a frown on his face the entire time she read KC's plea agreement. Every so often, she would glance up, giving him a frigid stare. KC looked to his lawyer to see if he had seen the look that Holloway had given him. He had talked to Holloway earlier that morning in her chambers. The lawyer patted him on his shoulder, reassuring him that everything was okay.

KC glanced around the courtroom one last time, still hoping that she would walk through the double doors. His heart skipped a beat after he saw the doors open up. To his disappointment, Detective Ramos came strolling in, stealing a seat in the back row. Their eyes met briefly. Ramos nodded, but KC turned away.

Judge Holloway took a sip of water before she began. "Mr. Carter, did you knowingly, and willfully sign this plea agreement?"

KC cleared his throat. "Yes, mam."

"Before we continue, is there anything the defense would like to say?"

"Yes, your honor," KC's lawyer said, standing up. "We would like to request a bond hearing as soon as possible."

"Denied. I don't give bonds on murder cases held in my court-room. Is that clear?"

"Yes, your honor." He took a seat.

Holloway took another sip of water. "Mr. Carter, I'm going to accept the terms of your plea agreement that the prosecutor has prepared. Just so you'll have some idea of the amount of time you'll be receiving, I'm gonna tell you. More than likely, you'll be receiving a sentence of ten years the next time we meet. However---"

"Fuck that!" the victim's brother yelled from the front tow. His sister grabbed his hand, trying to get him to sit back down. "Nah!" He snatched away from her. "If my brother can't see his kids again, he shouldn't either."

Holloway banged her gavel violently. "Order in my court-room," she demanded. "No more outbursts. Is that clear?" Their silence answered his question.

Out of the judge's view. KC threw up a Blood sign, on the sly, to the victim's brother. The man mouthed the words, "I'ma kill you," at him, before KC turned back around.

"Mr. Carter," Holloway proceeded, "You should consider yourself very lucky. You still have a chance to get out and live a productive life. So I suggest you take full advantage of the programs that the state has available for you. Who knows, maybe you could write a novel or something. Get you a deal with that guy named, *CA$H*, at *LockDown Publications*. That is all. Court is adjourned."

***

The minute KC got back to the county jail, he headed straight to the phone. He didn't know if she'd accept the call, but he tried his luck calling Tiffany's house, collect.

Her boyfriend, Ashton, answered. "Hello."

The operator came on. "You have a collect call from...KC. If you would like to accept, press five now."

Ashton pushed five.

"Ay, man, don't trip," KC said. "I'm Misty's boyfriend. I was just calling Tiffany because I haven't been able to catch up with Misty. I just want to ask her a few questions. That's all."

"It's cool." Ashton yelled. "Angie, pick up the damn phone!"

"Who is it?" she yelled back from the kitchen.

"Some nigga named KC or Kacey or some shit. Just pick up the phone."

Ashton hung up after he heard her pick up the other phone.

"How you doing, KC?" Tiffany said innocently.

"Wha'sup, man?" KC's voice as hostile. "Where's Misty? I've been calling her aunt's house, but she ain't never there. She didn't even show up for none of my hearings. How she just gonna run off on me like that?"

Tiffany felt sorry for him. She was responsible for some of his pain, persuading Misty to run out on him. KC was really in love with Misty, and she knew it. Instead of telling him the straight-out truth, she decided to pacify him with a good lie.

"KC, listen. That dude that you supposedly killed, his brother came around asking questions about Misty. We got scared thinking that he was gonna kill her, so she left town for a while. After she gets back on her feet, she's gonna send you some money and everything."

"You got a number or address to where she's staying?"

"I don't have it, but I can get it. It'll take me a while, though."

"A while?" he repeated. "Listen Tiffany, I'ma call you back in a couple of weeks. If you ain't got the information that I need to get in touch with her, including the address, consider your ass in the sling right along with hers." He slammed the phone down. "I can't believe this bitch," he said on the way to his cell.

***

Sitting Indian-style on the floor beside her bed, Misty counted all of the money she had been saving. She had been working for two months and only saved up three grand. It was good, considering her circumstances, but she needed more. She still needed a place to stay and a car to get around in. She was definitely gonna have to stop clubbing with Kylie so much.

So far, she liked Mobile and had plans to stay for good. It was a nice place for a girl like her to make a fresh start. She only wished that KC was there with her, instead of lying up in that white man's cage. After being ditched by Kylie last night, because she had a date with Keith, Misty really started to miss him even more.

She could imaging him lying on his bunk, staring out into space, wondering why she had done him the way she did. The thought made her stomach knot up. As soon as she got where she wanted to be, she would write him and send him a bankroll. Maybe even fly out there to visit him.

Someone knocked on her door. Quickly, she gathered up the bills, stuffing them into her dresser drawer. "Just a minute," she said, stalling whoever it was. Glancing around the room, making sure nothing personal was lying about, she opened up the door. P'Cola was standing there, holding a Taco Bell bag.

"I bought you something to eat. I know you're hungry after being asleep all evening."

"Thank you." She took the sack from him. "That was sweet of you."

"Do I turn you on?" he blurted out.

Misty smiled. "What?"

"Don't worry. Stacy went out with her friends." He stepped closer to her. "You can be honest."

"P'Cola, have you been drinking?" She could smell alcohol on his breath, now that he was in her space.

"Yep. I'm drunk off looking at you." He attempted to kiss her.

She put her hands on his chest, stopping him. You need to go take a shower P'Cola, then lie down until the liquor wears off."

P'Cola licked his lips. "I may be a little drunk, but I'm aware of everything. I'm aware that when a woman walks around a man's house in panties while his girl is away, she's either trying to give him some, or she's a fuckin' cock tease." He reached for her breast. "Now come on, before Stacy gets back."

Misty could see a hump growing in his pants. She wanted to reach down and caress it, but she remained in control of herself. Messing around with Stacy's man under the roof of her own house was bad karma. She'd rather continue playing the tease game, wearing skimpy clothes around the house.

"Stop it, P'Cola!" she said with authority.

He frowned, backing away from her. "A'ight. If you change your mind. I'll be in the shower." He left her standing there.

Slowly, she closed the door. She set the bag down, then dropped down on the bed, holding the pillow up to her chest. Her eyes focused on the ceiling while she thought. If she gave P'Cola some pussy, how would it benefit her? He seemed to be making damn good money at the shop. Looking at her new wardrobe and the way Stacy lived, he didn't mind sharing it. A good shot of pussy might be the key to his safe. It worked for Stacy. Besides, did she really give a damn if he was Stacy's man or not? That never stopped her before. It was settled. She would become P'Cola's live-in mistress until she got everything she needed to move on.

She got up off the bed. A quick peek out the window informed her that Stacy had not yet returned. She took off her T-shirt and panties and slipped into her robe. She left the room with a wicked smirk in her face. Just knowing that a dick was about to run up in her made her legs tremble.

Her plan to start a new life in Mobile was about to be ruined. No more playing. "Miss Nice Girl." Misty's usual conniving, sneaky self was about to come out. It was the only way that she would be able to get ahead quickly.

Steam filled the bathroom. Misty entered, tiptoeing, ready to surprise him with her naked body. Her robe fell to the floor, then she slid open the shower door. P'Cola looked shocked at the sight of Misty standing there, naked. His once limp organ stood and saluted.

Starting with her toes, he slowly ran his eyes up her olive-colored body. She had small breasts, and her pussy was shaven. She eyed him lustfully, licking her lips while he eye-fucked her body.

"Want me to wash it for you?" she asked in a sexy voice. She took the washcloth off the rack and lathered it with soap. The hot water ran down her silky mane, which stretched to her back. Gently, she ran the war, soapy washcloth over his large body. After she finished washing him, she pressed her body up against his, kissing him passionately on the lips. Her small hand made its way down between his legs and began to massage his dick. She sucked his lips and chest, biting down on his ripples downward. Her tongue stabbed his deep navel while she jacked him off.

He moaned while he impatiently waited on her to take him into her mouth. Dropping to her knees, she continued to stroke him while kissing his thighs and pelvis. His body began to squirm with pleasure. Her touch was soft and gentle. Her kisses came as close to his dick as they could, without touching it. She stopped suddenly, then stood up. "I don't suck dick for free," she said softly, then jammed her tongue into his ear.

P'Cola grabbed her ass, lifting her up. She reached down and grabbed his dick, then he slid her down on it while holding her up. "Shit!' she exclaimed, feeling her pussy stretch to the size of his dick. He hadn't been up in pussy that tight since Jenna's in his last year of high school.

She wrapped her legs around his big body, locking her feet. Holding onto the back of his head, she worked her hips back and forth and buried her face into his shoulder.

"AH! AH! AH! AHHH!" she hollered. "Yesss. Gimme that dick, daddy!" She switched to a circular motion. Her pussy was so wet it felt like she had turned on a faucet inside her.

"Mmm...shittt...I'm....I'm...cum...ming!" She dug her nails deep into his back as she grinded deeper on him. With one good thrust, she felt her vaginal fluid release all over his dick.

P'Cola was turned on even more because he had never experienced a pussy that came that hard. His plans to turn her around and get his nut doggy style were thwarted. "Unt unh. I'm not finished with you yet," she said into his ear. They got out of the shower dripping wet. She instructed him to sit down on the toilet, then she straddled him.

"Umph. Shit!" P'Cola gasped. Her pussy began to feel like she turned up the temperature. She popped her pussy on his shaft in a steady motion. She placed her feet flat on the floor, then started springing up and down on him like a frog. She leaned back, allowing P'Cola the full sight of her shaved pussy sliding up and down on his thick dick. While she worked on her second nut, P'Cola got a look at her weird facial expressions. Her mouth hung open and her eyes were wandering around inside her head. The sound of their skin slapping together could be heard over their loud moans.

P'Cola began to feel the need to release the nut he had reserved specially for her. He grabbed her by her tiny waist to support her, spread her pussy lips and began stroking her clitoris. Pumping into her with no reserve, he filled her pussy with his hot, thick liquid. Her legs began to shake, and her pussy began to spasm uncontrollably. She felt herself cumming again and sat all the way down, absorbing every inch and every drop of him. Breathing hard, she got up, scooped up her robe, then walked sheepishly to her bedroom. She hadn't been fucked that good in a long time. She collapsed on her bed, eyes closed, dripping with satisfaction.

She would wait until after Stacy came before she would get back into the shower, so Stacy would think that she'd been in her room sleeping while she was out. Not fucking her man.

Stacy stuck her key into the lock, opening up the front door. She stumbled in, dropping her Prada purse on the couch. She had one too many drinks, and a good fucking was all she needed to top off the night. Something smelled funny. From left to right, she looked, sniffing the air. Did she smell sex? Or was she just drunk and paranoid?

P'Cola was asleep when Stacy crept into the room. Rushing out of her dress and heels, she slid into the bed next to him. She ran her foot up and down his calf while kissing on her chest.

He unconsciously rolled away from her. His eyes fluttered open after he felt her warm saliva on his body. Damn! The last thing he needed was for Stacy to come home horny. After what he had just gotten from Misty, he really wasn't trying to fuck her. Her pussy was good, but she didn't know how to take control like Misty did.

"Baaby," Stacy whined. "I wanna do it." She grabbed his limp dick. "Want me to get it up?

"Stop, Stacy." He removed her hand. "I'm tired. I been on my feet all day."

She sat up in the bed with her mouth agape. "You tired?" Since when did you start being too tired to get your dick sucked?" She got out of the bed. Suspiciously, she glanced around their bedroom. She hoped that Misty hadn't been in her bed.

P'Cola wished she would hurry up and get her drunk ass to sleep. Stacy remembered the funny odor she smelled when she walked into the house."

"Y'all think I'ma fool," she said. "That funky cock bitch!" She stormed out of the room.

Misty jumped out of the bed when Stacy came barging in. Stacy's eyes grew big as saucers when she saw that Misty was naked. "No you didn't fuck my man in my house, bitch."

At first Misty was too shocked to respond. But hearing the word "bitch" brought her back to reality. She didn't want to get P'Cola in trouble, so she backed down.

"Stay, what the hell are you talking about?" Misty grabbed a big T-shirt out of her dresser and put it on.

"You know damn well what I'm talking about." Stacy's eyes were both red and watery. "You've been fuckin' my man."

Misty pursed her lips. "Bitch, don't nobody want your fat-ass man. He's cool, but he's not my type. Sorry!"

"Why you naked then, bitch?" Stacy stepped closer to her.

Misty defensively put her hand up. "Don't walk up on me, Stacy," she warned. "While we're arguing, give me three feet."

"This is my house," Stacy reminded her.

"And? You're still gonna respect me," Misty demanded. "Now, like I was saying, I just got out of the shower, then I passed out on the bed. That's why I'm naked."

Stacy's eyes sharpened as she contemplated stealing on Misty. Drunk as she was, she'd probably end up getting knocked out. Still giving her a hard stare, Stacy backed out of the room.

"That must've been that bitch's funk that I smelled," she said to herself on her way down the hall.

Misty was disgusted with herself for not kicking that bitch's ass. She swore that after this was all over, she would go upside Stacy's head. Couldn't no bitch get away with talking to her like that.

Von Diesel

CHAPTER 13

He had her legs over his shoulders, hammering his dick into her tight pussy. Her eyes were open, appearing to be staring at him, but she wasn't. While he was pounding her, he felt a strong hand grab him by the ankle, pulling him out of her. "Whaa---" he yelled.

The woman came to and her eyes focused in on her husband, standing over her lover with a shotgun pointed at him.

"Baby, noooo!" she screamed, reaching out for him. Her husband pulled the trigger.

Keith's eyes popped open. He woke up, panting and sweating all over his sheets. He looked to the left and saw Kylie sleeping soundly beside him. No husband, nor shotgun, was in sight. It had all been a dream.

He yawned as he got out of bed, stretching his long frame. Seeing the unopened package of Trojans on top of his dresser reminded him that he hadn't used one last night. He was drunk, but he remembered her saying something about now wanting to use a rubber. He shook his head, disgusted with how stupid he could be when he drank. Every player had his weakness, and his was Moet and Chandon.

Now that he was up and walking around, he felt a queasy feeling in his stomach. He went into the kitchen and fixed himself a glass of fruit punch. He drank slowly while he pondered what he was going to do on this sunny Saturday. He'd start by going to the barbershop for a fresh taper.

He woke Kylie, then went to take a hot shower. By the time he finished and dressed, she had taken care of her hygiene in the bathroom downstairs, put on her clothes and was sitting in the living room, reading the paper. She looked up at him through her soft green eyes, smiling when he walked into the living room. "You look," she complimented him. She puckered her lips for a kiss.

He gave her two quick kisses. "You hangin' out with me to-day?"

She nodded. "Yes." She put down the paper and stood up. "Hold on, before I forget." She took two crisp hundred-dollar bills out of her wallet and handed them to him. "Your monthly payment."

"Good lookin' out.'""He grabbed his key, activated the alarm and led her out the door.

Some changes were being made around P'Cola's Barber and Beauty. Kathea, the lead beautician, had lost her previous position to Misty. P'Cola had made up some excuse about some money coming up short. Instead of her beef being with him, she was furious with Misty. She had a bad feeling about Misty ever since P'Cola first brought her into the shop. All of her flirting and being friendly with everybody was just an act. There was about to be a lot of drama around the shop. Kathea would bet her life on it.

Misty nonchalantly moved her things over to Kathea's booth without saying one word to her. There were no apologies, no "I didn't know" or anything like that. Kathea gave her an evil glare while she plugged her hand-held dryers into the outlets.

Misty caught the glare out of the corner of her eye. She faced Kathea. "Is there a problem?"

"Sure is," Kathea confirmed, setting down the hair dryer.

P'Cola heard the altercation and jumped between them before it went any further. "Hold up! Y'all not about to tear up my shop." He turned to Kathea. "If you have a problem, take it up with me. Not Misty."

Kathea backed off. "This ain't over, bitch."

"You ain't trying to see me, Kathea." Misty smirked. "And don't forget to take your daughter's ugly-ass picture off my mirror."

"That's it," Kathea said. She tried to swing on Misty, but P'Cola caught her arm with his huge hand. Misty took advantage of the situation. She stepped forward while P'Cola had a hold on her and hit her in the face.

"Unt unh, P'Cola, let me go, "Kathea demanded, trying to pull away from him. A speckle of blood ran out of her right nostril. "This bitch done stole on me."

"I said, cut the shit!" he hollered. "I'm not gonna say it again, Misty." He gave her a serious, hard stare. Accepting defeat, Misty backed away, He asked Kathea, "You alright?"

"I'm cool." She kept her eyes locked on Misty. "You gon' let me go now?"

"'I don't want to more bullshit out of y'all in my shop. I'm dead fuckin' serious." He released his grip.

"You gon' get yours, bitch," Kathea warned.

"Silly-ass bitches," P'Cola said on his way over to his chair.

Kylie walked through the door, followed by Keith. She had a huge grin on her face as she led him over to meet Misty. She was cleaning out her sink when Kylie spun around, drawing her arm back, ready to swing. The sight of Kylie standing there made her catch herself.

"Girl, you almost got knocked the fuck out," Misty said, letting down her guard. "I done already stole on one muthafucka today."

"What the hell are you talking about?" Kylie quizzed.

"Never mind. Wha'sup?" Her eyes caught Keith, standing behind Kylie, and immediately recognized him as the guy in the Camaro. Once again, they exchanged predatory looks.

That's the girl who was driving P'Cola's truck, he thought. I know they ain't friends. Damn, I hate to have to break Kylie's heart. Because I gots to hit that.

Kylie looked from Misty to Keith. Their savage looks didn't go unnoticed.

"You two know each other?" she quizzed.

Keith said, "No. I mean...I think I've seen her around before. Haven't I?'

Misty shook her head. "Not that I know of," she lied. She didn't want her friend to suspect that she wanted her man. "You must be mistaking me for someone else. Anyway, I'm Misty." They shook hands.

"Keith," he said, noticing how soft her hand was. He wondered what her legs would feel like wrapped around him.

"Nice to meet you," Misty grinned as she turned around to finish what she was doing.

"Keith said to Kylie, "I'ma be over here gettin' my shit cut." He felt kind of silly after the way Misty had played him.

"Alright baby." She kissed him on the cheek."

His big ego was shot. He was sure Misty had remembered him from the stoplight. That wink she gave him had to have meant something. Something clicked in his mind. She was driving P'Cola's truck that day. That's the reason why she pretended not to have ever seen me. She couldn't be all up in my face while P'Cola was around. He would kick her ass out of the shop, he thought.

He sat in a chair beside Junebug, who was playing a game of chess with another older man.

"What's up, Junebug?" Keith said. They both were too busy to speak, so they just grunted. He watched Junebug mistakenly move his rook instead of getting his queen out of the way of the other man's bishop. "Bad move, Junebug."

Junebug cut his eyes at him. "What? Stay out of my business. I didn't make no--"

His voice trailed off as he watched his opponent capture his queen.

"Check!" the man said with a triumphant smile on his face.

Junebug smacked the table with the palm of his hand. "Damn!" He turned, facing Keith. "Why you wait...until after I made the move...before you said something?""

"Don't blame me for yo' fuck up, Junebug," Keith said.

"You shouldn't have said nothing in the first damn place. All you did was fuck up my concentration.

P'Cola cracked a smile, listening to Junebug's bullshit. "Cut the shit, Junebug! Y'all been arguing about that game all morning. Put that shit up." P'Cola took the cape off of a customer. "Pay up at the counter."

Star walked in carrying her barber's bag over her shoulder. She was wearing a blue KC Royals cap and jersey with a pair of baggy blue shorts that hung to her knees. Misty was the first person that she fixed her eyes on . Misty saw her and quickly turned away. Star smirked. She knew how Misty would act after her first bisexual experience. She'd seen it many times before.

She pimped her way over to Misty. Misty put her head down, pretending to be concentrating on mixing a relaxer.

"Wha'sup? "Star said. "You've been ignoring me lately."

"Look Star," Misty responded in a hushed whisper. "What we did was a one time thing and it will never happen again."

Star blushed. "Yeah, okay," she said angrily. She stormed over to the chair, almost knocking down a little boy.

"Damn, Star. Watch where the hell you going," P'Cola said. She ignored him and began unpacking her equipment.

Keith sat in the chair, thinking about how to come at P'Cola about Misty. From where he was sitting, he hadn't seen one sign that they even knew each other. But that was how two people acted when they were creeping on the down low. Then Keith remembered seeing her driving P'Cola's truck. Ah, that's it. She must be his little cousin or something.

"Ay, P'Cola?" Keith said.

"Close your mouth so I can get up under your chin," P'Cola instructed him. Keith remained still while P'Cola cut away the little hairs around his goatee. "You can talk now." P'Cola positioned the chair so that it was facing the mirror.

Keith turned his head from left to right, checking out the haircut. "Take the top down a little more."

"A'ight." P'Cola changed the guard. "What was it you was about to say?"

"What's up with you and Misty over there? Y'all fuckin' around or what?" Keith quizzed.

P'Cola became suspicious. "Why you ask that? I ain't never mentioned her to you."

"I saw her driving the Excursion the other day. You gotta be doing something with her if she ain't family."

P'Cola smiled. "Yeah. That's one of my new broads," he said proudly. "Fine. Ain't she?"

"Mm hmm," Keith agreed. "Where you get her from?"

"She's from Dallas." He wanted to impress Keith. "She's staying with me and Stacy."

"With you and Stacy?" Keith exclaimed. "What kind of shit y'all got going on at home?"

P'Cola explained the whole situation to him, not forgetting to mention what happened in the shower. Keith imagined the fuck faces that she made while P'Cola was up in her. Evidently P'Cola had fucked her good because she wasn't paying Keith any attention.

"She's more like a friend," P'Cola said. "You know what I'm saying? I'm just helping her get on her feet. As far as us fuckin', that's something that just happened."

"So, she's free game then?" Keith inquired. "Since y'all are just friends and all."

Right then P'Cola realized the mistake he had made. He had opened the door for Keith to try to move in on his territory. He wanted to kick himself for saying that they were just friends. It was too late to take it back. If he did, it would look like he was trying to handcuff the bitch.

P'Cola shrugged. "Yeah. If you can pull her, pull her. Shit, I got a bitch at the crib."

Keith stood up, dusting the hair off of his neck. "I don't want her," he lied. "It just fucked me up when I saw her driving your truck. I mean, I know you're a trick and all, but---"

"Nigga, fuck you."

Keith laughed as they shook hands. "Kylie, he called out. She ended her conversation with Misty and came running. "Pay the man, baby."

Kylie opened up her Prada wallet and took out twenty-five dollars. "Here, P'Cola." She handed the money to him. "You got my man lookin' all handsome and shit."

"Yo' man?" P'Cola chuckled. "Girl, how you fall in love so easily?"

Kylie playfully hit him on the shoulder. "Shut up."

P'Cola continued to laugh. "Girl, you know I'm just fuckin' with you."

110

"No he ain't," Ashley, another barber, said without looking up from the head that she was cutting.

She put her arms around Keith. "Forget them, baby. They just hatin' cause you my man."

Keith was growing tired of hearing her say "my man" in public. It was cool when no one was around, but out in the open, he had an image to uphold. Plus, he didn't want her to ruin his chances with Misty. He had fucked friends before, but if Misty thought that Kylie was in love with him, she might play even harder to get. Although, the look in Misty's eyes told him that she was all for self.

"I'ma holla at you later, P," Keith said, following Kylie out.

While Keith was going out. Blue was coming in. He walked straight to Lil' Ant's empty chair and took a seat. Lil' Ant put the cape around his neck.

"What can I do for you, playa?" Lil' Ant adjusted the glasses on his face. "You want a line and shave?"

Blue looked over at Misty, who had seen him walk in. Then he looked at Lil' Ant. "Cut this shit off my head. Give me a nice fade."

Misty smiled, shaking her head. Now he's cutting his hair off. He must really have a thing for me. Too bad, I'm still gonna turn him down. She winked at him, then went on about her business. As soon as he was through, she knew that he would come begging her for a date.

Forty minutes later. P'Cola handed Blue a mirror. Blue smirked his new tight-ass fade. The low cut brought out the brown in his eyes, too. It was a look he hadn't seen in quite a while. She couldn't possibly turn him down now.

He paid Lil' Ant, then casually strolled over to her station. Her eyes were locked on the head of an attractive young lady whose hair she was styling. She could feel him standing over her. He sucked his teeth, feenin' attention. She still didn't look up.

The fact that she was ignoring him frustrated Blue. "How long am I gonna have to stand her lookin' stupid before you acknowledge my presence?"

She looked up, appearing to be surprised. "Hi, Blue."

"Notice anything different about me?" He turned his head from side to side.

She shrugged. "No."

"Look again," he said. This time he rubbed the top of his head.

"Oh, you got a haircut," Misty said, as if she had just noticed. "I know you didn't do all that for me?"

"Sho' did. I'm trying to show you how much going out with you means to me."

She put one hand on his shoulder. "Listen, I should've just been straight up with you in the first place." She paused. "I think you're cute and all...but I don't want to go out with you."

He was crushed. She could've at least given him a sympathy date. Now he knew that it was all a game from the very beginning. She had succeeded in making a fool out of him.

"So, let me get this straight," he said. "First you have me change from braids to dreadlocks. Then you lead me to believe that I'd have a chance with you if I cut my hair. Now you saying that I never had a chance?"

The girl who was getting her hair styled looked at Blue. "You did all that for her? That is so sweet. I wish somebody would go through all that trouble for me."

He ignored her and said, "You thrive on playing with niggas' minds 'cause you think you like that. Bitch!"

"I'm a bitch?" Misty pointed at herself.

"Nah, you a ho-ass bitch."

"If I'm a bitch, yo' mama's a bitch, you trick-ass pussy," she said hotly. "I could've taken your broke ass for what little you've got but I spared yo' trick ass, because what you did was sweet. Nigga, if we was in Dallas your bitch ass would be leakin' for talking to me like that." She stepped to him, pointing her finger in his face.

P'Cola heard the commotion and grabbed his .38. Gun down at his side, he marched over to them.

"You got to raise up outta here, homie," P'Cola said. "Don't nobody get loud up in her but me."

Seeing the gun in P'Cola's hand, Blue humbled himself. "Yeah, alright." He bit down on his bottom lip. He gave her an evil glare while he slowly backed toward the door.

Kathea shook her head. the place was about to go to shit a lot sooner than she thought. Misty was trouble, and P'Cola acted like he was too blind to see it. She saw the way Misty looked at Keith. She hoped that Kylie would have enough sense to keep him away from her.

***

Marvin Cease blasted out of the jukebox. Middle-aged women danced with their too-cool husbands and sugar daddies to the rhythm of the blues. Stale cigarettes and old fish grease reeked through the whole joint. On weekends, the jukebox was replaced with a live band that sang old blues songs all night long. This was the place where Keith hung out when he wanted to get away from the young crowd and unwind over a few games of pool and a few beers.

Kylie chalked her stick while she eyed the table for her next shot. Keith sipped on a cold Corona, waiting for her to fuck up. They were playing for twenty bucks a game, and this was their second. He had let her win the first, missing every ball he shot. He planned to beat her out of a hundred dollars before they left. Teach her a lesson about trying to go up against him.

"Three in the side," she said, calling her next shot. She sank it. She set up for the nest. "Two to the five, in the corner." This time she missed. "Damn! I almost had you again."

He sat his beer down. "Watch out, lil' one. Let me show you how it's done." He chalked his stick. "Twelve ball, up in the corner." He sank it. Then he cleared the rest of the balls off the table without giving her a chance to shoot again.

At the end of their seventh game, she found herself down a hundred dollars. "You quit?" he asked.

"Mm hmm. I can't win." She sipped her Corona.

He laughed. "Pay up, then." He held out his hand while she handed over the money. "Always bait ya sucka," he said, smiling.

"So I'm a sucka now, right? We gon' see who the sucka gon' be tonight," she joked. "You gon' have a mouthful of pussy."

He put his arms around her waist and kissed her on the lips. "I hope it tastes as good as your kisses."

Staring up at him, she said, "Would you fuck my friend Misty?" She had been wanting to ask the question ever since they left P'Cola's.

Keith looked confused. "If you want me to."

"Keith, I'm serious. Would you, if she let you?"

He thought about it. "Nope," he lied with a straight face. "She doesn't even turn me on." He kissed her again. "You do."

They danced to the blues for a while, in silence. Then, "How come you don't want a picture of me like you have of everybody else?"

"Who's everybody?"

She toyed with the chain on his neck. "Everybody is the girls that I saw in all those pictures in your bottom drawer. You've got one of everybody but me. How can I be down?"

He grabbed her soft-ass cheeks. "You have to pop that pussy on me better than they did."

"Mmm," she moaned. "I love it when you talk to me like that." She grabbed his dick. "Let's get out of here." She took his hand and led him toward the exit.

"We're using a rubber tonight," he said, watching her ass bounce in front of him.

"You said that last night and look what happened."

"I was drunk."

"Well, I guess we're on our way to the liquor store then, 'cause I want to feel your meat up in me. Not no damn rubber."

114

CHAPTER FOURTEEN

Fabien pulled his Challenger into the care wash. He parked at the vacuums, and his chrome rims kept on spinning. He hopped out wearing sweats, a T-shirt and a pair of Nike flip-flops. He ran his hand over his wavy head while searching for the change machine. It was mounted on a wall, between the bays. His cell phone vibrated on his hip.

"Yeah," he answered.

"Wha'sup wit' it, nigga?" Keith said in a low voice.

Fabien inserted some ones into the change machine. "What the hell you whispering for?"

"I'm in the bathroom. I got this bitch in my bed and I don't want her to hear me."

"Aw, yeah?" Fabien smiled. "Anybody I know?"

"Naw, nigga. Fuck all that. I gotta tell you about this new broad that I'm scoping on."

Fabien put the change into his pocket on the way back to the truck. "I'm listening."

Keith told him about Misty.

While he was listening, Stacy's Chrysler pulled into the car wash. She parked next to him at the vacuums. Instantly he remembered her from P'Cola's shop. She was looking good with her blond hair braided to the back in four braids.

Fabien said, "So you think P'Cola is tricking off with this broad? Just be careful, dog, I don't want y'all to end up gettin' into it over her. I got a hundred saying that she don't give you no play."

"Bet. I'll holla at you later."

Fabien put the phone back on his hip.

The Chysler door opened and Stacy got out, stretching her long legs. Reaching to her thigh, she pulled down her tight short-shorts. The yellow wife-beater she was wearing exposed the tattoo of her name and P'Cola's name on her upper arm. Taking off her glasses, she squinted from the bright sun while looking for the change machine.

That gave Fabien reason to approach her. "You lookin' for change?"

She looked at him. "Don't I know you from somewhere?"

He smiled, letting his diamonds reflect the sun. "Yeah. I saw you up at P'Cola's. Remember?"

"Yeah. He's my man," she said proudly.

"Yo' man?" he said, playing dumb. "I didn't know y'all was like that."

Stacy pointed a freshly manicured nail at him. "Now I remember. You're the little dude who was laughing at my baby because I didn't bring his lunch."

He leaned up against his truck. "What was I laughing for?"

"You were laughing and calling him a trick 'because I was late getting there," she reminded him. "Don't act like you don't know."

"I was probably laughing because I was jealous."

She looked confused. "Jealous of what?"

He licked his lips. "Cause he had your fine ass bringing him lunch. If you were mine, I'd be the one bringing the lunch." He looked her up and down. "I could get full just looking at you."

Her eyebrows shot up when she smiled. "I am like that, ain't I?" she bragged. She stepped back on her left leg, placing one hand on her hip. "Wait a minute. I know you ain't tryin' to holla?"

Standing straight up, he said, "Would I be wrong if I was?"

Slowly, he began walking around her, making a circle. "What if I told you...that your man, P'Cola..."he looked at her ass and imagined what it would feel like in his hands. "...was fuckin' that girl he got staying with y'all?" His eyes concentrated on the mound between her legs, and instantly he felt an erection swelling. "And...that she's in charge of the beauty shop? Would I be wrong for telling you that?" He stopped, stared into her eyes and waited for his words to sink in.

Her body twitched and tears began to roll down her cheeks. Quickly, she put her hands up to her face so he couldn't see her crying. Collapsing into the seat of her car, she began to weep.

"You didn't have to tell me that." She wiped her face with the back of her hand. "Don't you think I suspected it? I knew, I was just hoping that the bitch would leave soon so things could go back to normal.

Touching her chin, he turned her face toward his. She looked even better crying.

"I wouldn't waste my time crying over him." He was setting her up for the kill.

"What you think I should do?"

"Move on," he said in a serious voice. "you can't let him treat you like a fool because he got money." He wiped the rest of the water from under her eyes with his thumbs. "Find somebody that'll make you feel good inside. you walk around like you're stress free, but I can see that you're hutting.

Still sniffling, she looked up at him. "Why don't you take me out? You seem to have all the right answers."

He shook his head disapprovingly. "P'Cola's a friend of mine. Much as I want to, I can't--"

"I can tell that you want me," she said, interrupting him, "By the way you're looking at me." She sniffled, looking down at her legs. "I don't want to leave him. But I do want to get even."

Looking down at the top of her head, he said, "If we do, it'll have to be on the super down low. Can't nobody...I mean nobody know."

Her head slowly lifted. "That's exactly how I would want it."

Fabien pulled out his wallet, took out his business card, then handed it to her. "Give me a call when you're ready."

She took it. "I will."

"I'd love to see you in a thong, running around on some exotic beach."

A smirk appeared on her face. "Be careful what you wish for. You joist might get it," she said in a sexy tone. She was feeling better already.

Stacy put her legs inside her car and closed the door. She no longer felt like washing it.

"Call me," Fabien said as he backed away.

Smiling, she waved goodbye as she pulled off. Keeping her eyes on the road, she picked up her glasses and put them on. If P'Cola was gonna fuck around with another bitch, she could fuck around, too. Fabien had gotten her spirits back up by telling her how she deserved to be treated. She looked at the business card that he had given her.

Two businessmen are better than one, she told herself. I'll let him hit it a few times and see if it pays off. P'Cola will get suspicious of us and become jealous, then he'll be begging for me to stop. By that time, Fabien will be sprung and then they'll be bidding on this. She had to pat herself on the back for coming up with such a brilliant plan. She hopped into the right lane, then sped up, "I've got the Midas touch," she sang. "Everything I fuck turns to gold."

CHAPTER FIFTEEN

The warm shower water rolled down his muscular back, soothing his aching muscles. Eyes closed, he stood with his hands on the tile, enjoying the sensation. KC quietly uttered a prayer, asking God to somehow help him out of the mess that he'd gotten himself into. When he signed his plea agreement, he made sure that he kept his appellate rights open.

For a brief moment, Misty's face had flashed inside his mind. He was lonely without her. Almost every minute of the day was spent wondering what she was doing, and who she was with. He wanted an explanation for her leaving him the way she did.

He stepped out of the shower to dry himself off. It was almost count time, so he had to hurry. He had an important call to make. It had been two weeks since he talked to Tiffany. She should know something by now.

After he put on his orange jumpsuit and shower shoes, he hurried to the phone. Normally he wouldn't wear shower shoes to the phone, for fear that a fight might break out. But with count time being only ten minutes away, he took a gamble that nothing would jump off.

Using his sleeve, he wiped the germs off the receiver and dialed Tiffany's number. While he impatiently waited for an answer, a guy walked past him with headphones around his neck, blasting *Shit Crazy* by Gucci Mane. He smiled to himself, thinking that the song was appropriate for his current situation.

Tiffany had her home stereo system up loud, blasting R&B music while she cleaned her house. She thought that she heard the phone ringing, so she rushed to turn it down. On the coffee table she set down her Pledge and dust rag, then picked up the phone.

"Hello, she said, breathing hard. She waited until the operator finished announcing KC, then pushed five.

"You got that information for me?" he asked rudely. He didn't bother with the hellos and shit.

"Damn!" Tiffany exclaimed. "Can't you speak first? KC, I haven't done nothing to you."

"My fault," he said, apologizing. "How you doing, Tiffany?"

"Fine," she replied. "I found out that she's staying in Mobile, Alabama. She got a job doing hair at Ashton's cousin's coup, and she's doing alright."

"Mobile, Alabama? How she end up in Bama?"

"I told you, that dude's brother came around trippin' and shit," she lied. "She had to disappear." She didn't want him to know that she was the real reason why Misty left.

"You lying, Tiffany," he said angrily. "You said that she works for Ashton's cousin, P'Cola. She didn't just happen to meet him. Somebody told her about him and I think that somebody was you." He glanced around to see if anyone was listening to his conversation. A fat white man, who was waiting on the phone, was staring directly at his mouth. "Find yo' fat ass another place to stand," KC snapped on him.

"I ain't trying to lose my place," the fat man said.

"I don't give a fuck. It's almost count time anyway. So go to your cell." He watched the scared man mope away. "Back to what I was saying, Tiffany." His voice was calm but serious. "If by some miracle I get out soon, I'ma holla at yo' ass just as soon as I take care of her."

"Alright, KC. Damn!" Tiffany gave up. "She's staying with P'Cola and his girl. She's gonna write you as soon as she gets on her feet. That's what she said and that's all I know."

"Gimme the number," he demanded.

Tiffany sighed. She deeply regretted letting herself get caught up in the middle of this bullshit. "Let me call and see if you can have it, 'cause I don't want P'Cola to trip--"

"Gimme the fuckin' number, Tiffany," he demanded.

She took a deep breath, sick of his temper. "Hold on." She picked up her cell phone and scrolled through her contacts for P'Cola's number. "It's area code two five one---" she finished giving him the number, all the while hoping she wouldn't regret it.

He repeated the number, making sure that he got it right. After she confirmed it, he hung up the phone and ran to his cell to write it down. Immediately after count was over, he ran back to the phone.

The fat white man had come back, too. "Hey, I was next," he complained.

KC gave the man an evil stare. The man threw his hands in the air in defeat, then walked away. He had taken a beating over the TV the night before and didn't think he could take another one.

***

P'Cola stood in his driveway talking to his neighbor when his phone rang.

"Hello." Unbeknownst to him, Stacy had picked up the phone also.

The operator came on the line, announcing KC. P'Cola pushed five. "Who dis?"

"KC. Can I speak to Misty?"

"KC who?"

"I'm Misty's boyfriend."

P'Cola stepped away from his neighbor so he couldn't be heard. "Look here, man. I don't know how you got this number, but you can't call here any more. You ain't got no girl here."

"Stop playing games, man," KC pleaded. "I just want to talk to her."

"You don't understand," P'Cola said. "That's my girl now. So whatever y'all had is over with." He hung up.

Stacy hung up as well. She shook her head. "Trick-ass nigga," she said slowly. "I don't know why I even--" She began to cry. She knew everything, but actually hearing it out of his mouth was a blow to her heart.

She put her face in her hands. After a few minutes of crying, she remembered that Fabien's card was in her purse. She found her purse and took the card out of her wallet. "I'ma show his ass how to play games since he thinks I'm some damn fool."

She quickly put the card back into her purse after she heard P'Cola come into the house. He walked into the bedroom. Stacy was standing in front of the dresser, pretending to fix her hair.

"Stacy," he said, "run down to the phone company and get the number changed."

No he didn't, she thought. He likes this bitch so much, he's about to change the phone number so her real man can't call. She was so enraged that she wanted to throw something at him. But she kept her cool.

"Why not just call the phone company?" she said evenly.

"Because if you go down there, they'll get right on it."

She knew he was getting rid of her so he could question Misty about KC.

"Ride with me," she said, fucking with him. "We don't spend no time together."

"I can't. I gotta finish washing my truck." He pulled a couple of hundred-dollar bills out of his wallet and handed them to her. "It shouldn't cost too much."

Stacy snatched her purse off the dresser. Her insides were on fire. I'm gonna have the last laugh, she thought as she walked away. He's gonna pay for this shit.

P'Cola walked outside with her and gave her an obligatory peck on the lips. He then picked up the soapy rag out of the bucket and started washing the wheels. He could see her Mustang pulling away out of the corner of his eye. After waiting a few minutes to make sure she was gone, he dropped the rag, then went into the house.

Misty was lying across her bed in a pair of pajamas, reading Hard and Ruthless, when P'Cola barged into her room.

She sat up. "Don't you know how to knock?

"I don't knock on doors inside my own house," he said smartly. He forced her legs out of his way, then sat on the bed next to her.

She could easily tell that he was disturbed by something. He had never used that tone with her before.

"What's up, baby?" She put her hand on his leg.

He pushed her away. "Who the fuck is KC? And how come I don't know about him? But best of all, why is he callin' my phone?"

Misty was confused. How in the hell did KC get his number? she thought.

"You still want that dude or what?" he quizzed.

She took his hand, rubbing it gently. "Baby, KC was my boyfriend when I stayed in Dallas. I have no idea how he got your number, but I'm gonna find out."

P'Cola thought back to something that Misty said to Blue when they were arguing at the shop. He remembered her saying, "If we were in Dallas, yo' trick ass would be leaking for talking to me like that." And for the first time he wondered what she was doing in Dallas in the first place.

P'Cola said, "What made you leave Dallas? And what happened between you and ole boy?"

She sighed, pushing her back out of her face. She told him that KC killed a man that tried to rape her. The only reason she left was because she feared retaliation from the man's family. The only truthful thing that she told P'Cola was that she cut ties with KC to get on with her life.

Misty massaged his neck. "I was gonna get in contact with him after I got back on my feet," she admitted. "But then I met you." She pulled his face towards hers, jamming her tongue into his mouth. He was upset, and she wanted to give him something to soothe him.

Because of him, her stash was up to ten grand and he was gonna give her the cash to buy a new car. She got up, walked over to the window and closed the shades. Teasingly, she removed her shirt, showing him her hard nipples.

"Do we have time for a quickie before wifey gets back?" she asked seductively. She dropped her pajama bottoms and panties to the floor, then got into bed.

She grabbed her ankles and held up her legs, giving him a peek at what she had waiting for him. With no time for foreplay, P'Cola quickly pulled down his pants and positioned himself between her legs. He hit her with fast, deep strokes, wanting to punish her because of KC. Loudly she moaned, not only to boost his ego and clear his mind of KC, but also because his deep stroke was hitting her just right.

The phone rang.

Misty's warm crevice was too good for him to pull out, but it might've been Stacy, so he had to answer it. Reaching over, he picked the phone up off the small table that stood next to her bed.

"hello," he said between breaths. Misty continued to move her hips in a circular motion, watching the funny faces he was making. He couldn't help but smile when he heard the operator announce KC. P'Cola pushed five, then said, "Hold on right quick." He sat the phone down on the pillow next to Misty's face.

"Ooh! Ooh, ooh, OHH, shiiit!" Misty cried out after P'Cola began hammering her again. She knew that someone was on the phone, she just thought he was showing off for one of his friends. So she went ahead and put on a show. "Yes, daddy!' she hollered. "Ah, it's so big!"

P'Cola stopped suddenly on the down stroke. Picking up the phone, he said, "I told you nigga, that's my bitch!" Then he hung up.

Misty peeped game right away. She pushed him off of her. "Who was that on the phone?"

He avoided eye contact. "What you talkin' about?" P'Cola played dumb, but the guilty look on his face told her everything she needed to know.

Getting out of the bed, she threw her panties into the hamper, then slipped into her robe. After she finished, she looked up at him. "Please don't tell me that was KC."

He looked stone-faced.

She put her hand up to her forehead. "I can't believe you, P'Cola!" she yelled. "What kind of player are you? You didn't have to do him like that. Damn!"

"No, you didn't have to do him like that," he said defensively. "You're the one who left him after he went to jail behind yo' ass."

She frowned. "Get the fuck outta my room, P'Cola!" She pointed at the door.

"Aw'ight." He pulled up his pants.

Through all the commotion, they didn't hear Stacy walk into the house. When P'Cola opened up Misty's room door, he saw Stacy coming down the hallway. Seeing him coming out of Misty's room caught her off guard and she froze for a brief moment. When reality kicked back in, she stormed toward the room. His mouth dropped open as he backed up. Misty was standing next to her bed with an angry look on her face when Stacy barged in.

Suspiciously, Stacy looked back and forth at the two guilty faces. "What's going on?" she said evenly.

"Tell her, P'Cola," Misty said, about to give him a taste of his own medicine.

"Yeah," Stacy said, "tell me P'Cola."

"I don't know what the hell she's talking about," he said unconvincingly. Stacy knew too much of his business and could get him into serious trouble with the law if she chose to.

Misty said, "Your man came in here trying to get some pussy."

P'Cola and Stacy were both shocked at what she had just said. Stacy was confused. She thought they had already fucked. Now Misty stood here saying that he was only "trying" to get some pussy.

Stacy closed her eyes and asked, "P'Cola, what's going on?" She would have been furious if she hadn't just had a juicy conversation with Fabien on her way home.

"She's lying," P'Cola argued. "I just came in here to see if she had seen the remote to the TV." His brain didn't work fast enough to come up with a good lie.

"The remote to the TV?" Stacy grunted. With her arms folded across her chest, she glanced at Misty. "I need to talk to you in our room, P'Cola."

P'Cola quietly walked past her to their room down the hall. "I remember when I first met you," she said to Misty. "you told me that I didn't have to worry, because you didn't want my man."

"And I still don't," Misty replied hotly.

Stacy's arms fell down to her sides. "Hurry up and get your shit together 'cause I want you out of my house, tonight."

"Fine with me, bitch," Misty said harshly. "I don't want to stay here no way." She picked up the phone and called Kylie.

"Hello," Kylie answered in a groggy voice.

"Come pick me up," Misty demanded. I'm at P'Cola's. Hurry up because they're over here trippin'."

"I'm on my way," Kylie said. "Do I need to bring my .22?"

"Nah," Misty said, eyeing Stacy, who was standing in the doorway, watching her. "If this bitch gets out of line, I'ma drag her ass out in the street and beat the shit out of her." Misty hung up the phone, then immediately began packing her stuff. Stacy was still standing in the doorway watching her. "You ain't got to watch me. I been ready to get the fuck out of here."

Stacy rolled her eyes as she turned to walk away. "Don't let the door hit you in the ass on the way out!" she yelled over her shoulder.

Misty went into the closet and grabbed her small Sentry safe where she kept the ten grand she had saved up. She stuffed her clothes into the suitcases that P'Cola bought her and carried them to the front door. She heard Kylie pull up outside, blowing her horn. Misty went back to her room to make sure that she hadn't left anything. Then she left.

***

At Kylie's apartment, Misty made a nice, comfortable pallet on the living room floor. Kylie's place was small but clean and nicely furnished. Curling irons, combs and cosmetics were scattered about inside the bathroom. It was a typical place for a young woman who lived alone.

After Misty washed P'Cola's smell off of her, Kylie showed her around so she could find the kitchen in the dark if she got hungry in the middle of the night. Misty noticed something during the short tour--a picture of Keith was in every room of the apartment, except for the closets. That was gonna be hard for her to get used to, especially since he looked so much like KC.

Still sleepy, Kylie went back to bed, leaving Misty by herself. She picked up Keith's picture off the TV, then curled up on the floor, examining it. She wondered if he was anything like KC. Was he tough and willing to do anything for his woman? Speaking of KC, he was probably ready to kill her. how could she blame him? Especially after that stunt P'Cola pulled. That had to have done more than just break his heart. It must have cut it in two. Somehow she was gonna find a way to set things straight with him.

She got up, setting the picture back on the TV. If she would have fallen asleep with it and gotten caught by Kylie, she wouldn't have anywhere to go. After a while, her eyes closed and she drifted off into a deep sleep, putting the horrible day behind her.

***

After P'Cola hung up in his face, KC stormed back to his cell. His cellmate was sitting on his bunk reading the newspaper when he came in cussing and yelling.

"Trifling-ass bitch!" he yelled angrily. Breathing hard, he stared at his reflection in the mirror. His face was beet red and his eyes were narrow slits.

The power of a woman. His face balled up as he punched the mirror with his fist. Blood ran from his knuckles while he stood over the face bowl, looking down at them. His breathing began to slow as his temper cooled. Over and over, his ears played back Misty's heart-stabbing moans of passionate lovemaking. The exact same sound that he'd heard many times in their bedroom. Now, she was performing the same song for another man.

"I'm a goddamn fool," he said slowly.

His cellmate was an older man, around fifty-five. Day after day he went to the law library trying desperately to get back the forty-five year sentence that he had received. He was a big, bald man with a long salt-and--pepper colored beard. He removed his glasses and wiped his eyes with the sleeve of his shirt.

"What's wrong, son?" he asked. KC had a look on his face that he knew was caused by a woman.

He had done two bids before this one and had seen it all. He knew that there were only two things that could drive a man to hurting himself inside the joint like he had seen KC do with the mirror. One was a death in the family, and the other was the lost love of a woman.

KC respected no one, but for some reason he felt close to his celly, Slim Vegas. During a time of loneliness and abandonment he thought how one unconsciously became close to another sharing the same troubles.

"Ain't nothin' wrong," KC answered. He turned the faucet on and stuck his bloody hand under it. Then he wrapped it up with a towel and climbed up on his bunk. For a moment he said nothing. Then, he finally spoke up. "Man, this bitch," he said sadly.

Slim Vegas said, "I keep on telling you brother, you've got to rid your mind of that problem. Here it is, you done caught a case for her and haven't heard from her since you've been here." He shook his head, disgusted by KC's hard-headedness. "Let her go, young bro. She's only gonna bring you down."

KC put his face into the palms of his hands. Getting out of there was on his mind. He decided that the best and only thing for him to do was get in the law library and hope for a miracle. He hoped that there were some discrepancies in his case that his public defender may have overlooked.

"What time does the library open tomorrow?" he inquired.

By then, Slim Vegas was back into his newspaper. He closed it and put it down on the bed. He stood up and faced KC on the top bunk. "Noon. Why?"

"I think I'm gonna take your advice," KC said. "I'ma start putting all of my energy into trying to get out of here. Fuck lying around, stressin' all the time."

Slim Vegas smiled. "That's what I'm talking about, young brother. Tomorrow we'll go down there together."

Von Diesel

CHAPTER SIXTEEN

Tick. Tick. Tick.

The second hand on Keith's clock turned slowly while he sat staring at it. He was waiting for the clock to hurry up and strike six. It had been a long day and he was ready to go home, call Jocelyn and call it a night.

He checked the calendar on his desk to make sure that it was Jocelyn's turn to be with him tonight. Yep, Jocelyn was the lucky girl. He hadn't been with her in a while and figured that she was overdue for a good tune-up. Jocelyn was a good source of income, but he knew his constant neglecting her would soon run her off. The best thing for him to do was to dedicate the whole week to her, put her portrait up in the living room and put a few of her belongings inside of his drawers. Then she would start feeling special again. A smile appeared on his face while he thought about how she liked to be choked during sex. Then he imagined her sitting in front of him with a short bob haircut with long ass lashes. He loved that big smile she wore, no matter what was going on in her life. She was smart, too. He was sure that someday she would make some lucky man a fine wife.

Devontae barged into his office, interrupting his thoughts. "Wha'sup," he said, taking a seat.

"Shit. What's up with you?"

"Finally finished during the paperwork on the new Rams that came in last week." He picked a piece of lint off his slacks. "You pull that ho yet?"

Keith regarded him curiously. "Who?"

"The bitch that was driving P'Cola's truck. You know damn well who I was talking about."

Keith waved a hand at him. "No, but you can go ahead and add her to my stable. Trust me, she's as good as got," he said confidently. He got an idea in his head. "As a matter of fact, we ought to go out tonight." The very mention of Misty made him forget about Jocelyn completely.

"I'm cool wit' that."

"Good. Because I'ma ride with you."

Keith picked up the phone, calling P'Cola at the barbershop.

"P'Cola's Barber and Beauty." he answered professionally.

"What's up with you, big dog?"

"Finishing up on my last customer's head."

Keith leaned back in his chair. "We thinkin' about stepping out tonight. I was calling to see if you wanted to meet up with us at the club."

P'Cola stepped away from the man whose hair he was cutting. He was checking his hairline to see if it was straight. "Yeah, I guess. I ain't doing nothin' else. What time y'all going?"

"Keith looked up at the clock. "Round ten."

"Count me in." P'Cola hung up.

Keith hung up the phone with a devious look on his face. He called P'Cola to come along, only because he knew that P'Cola would bring Misty, trying to show her off. That's when he'd make his move on her. After all, P'Cola said that she was just a friend. He couldn't hate on Keith for wanting a piece, too.

After he finished talking to P'Cola, he called Jocelyn, telling her that he would see her after the club. Devontae and Keith both got up and left the office. It was time to go home. On their way out of the front door, they saw Jason coming out of his office. He had a fine-ass black girl in tow.

"Keith, Devontae, what's up, yo?" Jason said cheerfully, walking past them. "That shit you told me really works."

To both of their surprise, the attractive girl paid them no mind at first. A few feet away, the attractive girl said, "Don't hate, don't hate," over her shoulder.

"Damn!" Devontae said. "What did you tell 'em?"

"Man, he bought that bitch. Why you think she didn't drool after she saw us? He's a John. Keith chuckled.

"You just hating 'cause you haven't pulled Misty's fine ass yet." Devontae walked off.

"I promise I'ma make you eat them words."

***

Keith stepped out of the shower and dried himself with a blue Polo towel. He slapped on some cologne, then applied some Dax wave grease to his head. He then opened up his closet, unveiling a row of expensive suits of all colors and styles. He selected a tan pinstripe Armani suit, a cream-colored shirt and tie and a pair of cream-colored gators. To add a little pizzazz, he put on his diamond-studded white gold watch, a white gold diamond pinky ring and a pair of personalized cufflinks.

Adjusting his tie, he eyed himself in the full-length mirror that hung on the outside of the closet door. God knows he created a work of art when he made me, he thought. He snapped his fingers remembering to put Jocelyn's portrait up and scatter some of her belongings about. He'd wait until after he left the club before he called her. Who knows, he thought. I might end up leaving with Misty.

He had just finished hanging Jocelyn's portrait when he heard Devontae's car pull into his driveway. Checking the mirror one last time, he realized that he'd forgotten his earrings. He ran to his bedroom, got the earrings, secured his house and walked out the door.

Devontae blew his horn impatiently as he sat in his Silver Challenger on chrome twenties. He let off the horn when he saw Keith walking toward the car.

"Hurry yo' ass up!" Devontae yelled. "Don't forget your VIP card."

Keith stopped suddenly. "Damn!" He ran back inside the house. From his kitchen drawer, he took out the gun that he had gotten from Fabien. He stuck it in his waist. Devontae was fuming by the time he got back to the car.

"You's a slow muh-fucka." Devontae said. "Takin' all night and shit."

"Fuck you!" Keith said, getting in. "I forgot my strap." He took it out and put it inside the glove box.

Devontae frowned. "What you need that for?"

Keith let the seat back, making himself comfortable. "Shut up and drive, simp." The gun was making him feel powerful already.

Devontae sighed and put the car into reverse, backing out the driveway.

***

Earlier that day, after P'Cola closed down the barbershop, he flew out to Dauphin Street to Kylies' apartment, looking for Misty. He parked his truck next to Kylie's, then ran up to her door. Kylie answered wearing a pair of gray sweats and a white T-shirt. She had a disgusted look on her face after she saw that it was P'Cola.

"We took the day off," she said smartly.

"Man, where Misty at?" Kylie's large breasts, bulging through her shirt, did not go unnoticed by P'Cola.

She saw him staring at them and folded her arms across her chest." She ain't here," she lied.

"Cut the bullshit, Kylie."

"I said she ai---"

"Who is it, Kylie?" Misty interrupted as she appeared behind Kylie. She frowned after her eyes fixed on P'Cola.

He said, "Can I talk to you for a minute?"

"For what?" To tell you the truth, I'm not feeling you right now, P'Cola."

He looked at Kylie, who was staring down his throat. "Can you leave us alone? Please!? he said smartly. "Ain't Keith callin?"

Kylie rolled her eyes as she turned to leave. "Whatever," she said over her shoulder. She wanted to cuss his ass out, but she kept in mind that she worked in his shop. She couldn't afford to get fired.

Misty stepped out on the porch, closing the door behind her. "What do you want? I hope that you're here to apologize; otherwise, you can leave now."

"I'm sorry," he pleaded.

She shook her head. "Unt unh, nigga. That ain't gonna work. You've got to say it like you mean it."

He sighed. "Aw'ight, damn. I'm sorry, Misty. Is that better?" He looked around, then whispered. "Girl, you tryin' to make a playa like me look bad. I hope ain't nobody watchin'."

She pointed her finger at him. "See, that's your problem. You like to front too much."

He stepped closer to her, his face almost touching hers. "Gimme kiss."

Gently, she pushed him away from her. "Kiss Stacy. She's the one you're in love with."

"Come on man. Don't even go there. Slowly, but sho'ly, you're stealing my heart. Why you think I'm here?"

"Prove it."

"What I'm doing ain't proof enough?"

She shook her head.

"How can I prove it?" he inquired.

Misty placed her hand on his chest, running it up to his head, pulling his face towards hers. She kissed him on the lips passionately. He grabbed her ass and pulled her against his body. When she felt his swollen manhood against her pelvis, she moved away.

I'm gonna miss your sweet kisses," she said.

She stared at him for a moment. The silence kept him in suspense. "It will be," she finally spoke, "if you do a little somethin' somethin' for me. If you like me like you say, it shouldn't be a problem for you to take care of your mistress' needs."

He liked that. Saying that she was his mistress made him feel like she had accepted her place as being second in his life.

"What do you need me to do?" he asked curiously.

"I need some money to get a car," she said. "What good does it do me to be second in your life if I can't get anything out of it? I mean, shit, if I'm gonna be your mistress, you're gonna treat me like one."

"P'Cola thought about it for a moment. Was she worth all of the money he had been giving her lately? He thought about all the times they had snuck around the house to fuck while Stacy was asleep. She used to cover her mouth with her panties so Stacy couldn't hear him moaning while she rode him on the laundry room floor. Yeah, she was worth it.

Three young dudes in a candy-apple red Impala on gold Daytons rode past, staring at Misty. She sneakily glanced at the driver, who winked at her. He was sitting low, with his ball cap cocked to the left and one hand on the steering wheel. P'Cola saw her looking around him, so he turned around to see what had her attention. They threw up Blood signs at him, hoping he would bite. He didn't.

"I'll tell you what," he said, turning around. Misty gave him her attention once again. She only looked at the dude in the Impala to make P'Cola jealous. "Let's go out tonight and I'll let you know tomorrow."

With a wave of her hand, she said, "Ain't no thinking about it. Either you're gone do it or you're not. I can always find someone who will." She shrugged. "That's alright. Keith said that he would hook me up if I came to see him. So, Im cool."

He stroked his chin. "Keith, huh?" P'Cola shook his head. He knew the game she was playing, but he couldn't help but admire her style. If he would've known that them Texas broads were like that, he would've moved out there a long time ago.

"Aw'ight," he agreed. "I'll give you enough for a down payment. Is that cool with you?"

She smiled triumphantly, revealing a set of white teeth. When she was happy, her eyes became narrow slits that went halfway to her ear. "That'll do. Now, where we going tonight?"

"We are going to The Gentlemen's Club."

"Who is we?"

"Me and a couple of my boys. Bring Kylie with you."

"Alright. We'll be there."

"Cool." He leaned toward her, trying to get a kiss.

She stopped him. "Don't push it. You're still in the dog house."

He backed up, throwing his hands in the air in mock surrender. "I'll just see you later, then."

136

On the way back to his truck, he heard her say. "I love you!" Then she went back inside. Even a thousand miles away from home, she could still work her magic.

Von Diesel

CHAPTER SEVENTEEN

The Gentlemen's Club parking lot was packed with expensive SUVs and cars of all types. It was a classy place, so you rarely saw girls prancing around with their asses hanging out, flagging down expensive cars. Royals, Chiefs and boss players graced the place with their patience when they wanted to have a good time within the city limits.

The line to get into the club stretched all the way around the building. Keith and Devontae got a good look at all the fine honeys while they made their way to the front of the line with their VIP cards.

When they walked in, the dance floor was crowded with people doing the Cha Cha Slide. They grooved to the beat of the music on their way over to the VIP section. Devontae caught sight of a tall, chocolate, thick-in-the-hip girl with a long weave, staring a hole through him. He winked at her, acknowledging her presence, but kept on walking.

They took a seat at a table that overlooked the dance floor. Keith motioned for the waitress to bring a bottle of his usual.

"It's some hoes up in here," Devontae said, looking around. Women were at the bar, playing pool and sitting on laps. It was like a convention. "You might have to find you another ride home."

"You been talkin' real slick at the mouth lately," Keith said.

"I've got the game and gone with it."

Keith smiled at his protege. "Play on, playa."

The DJ played Lil' Boosie's new song." Keith took off his jacket and gave it to the girl in the coat check room. He hoped she wouldn't hold it hostage just to get next to him. He was on a mission tonight and didn't have time to get side-tracked. He had a gut feeling that Misty would be in the house tonight.

"I see two freaks on the floor waiting on us," Keith said. "Let's get on 'em."

Devontae followed him onto the dance floor where they came in on two redbones who were dancing with each other. Keith slid up behind one of them, grinding on her butt like he knew her. Instead of stopping him, she went on with the flow. Devontae was slower to approach the other one, but soon they were all over each other.

Keith was all up on her, whispering in her ear. She smiled and squirmed from his breath tickling her neck. Suddenly, he felt a strong hand grab his shoulder. "Get off my woman!" he heard someone say.

The man spun around him. He was relieved to see that it was only P'Cola. Laughing at Keith's expression, P'Cola said, "Man, let's go sit down and have a drink. You'll have plenty of time to fool around with these tramps later." Keith noticed that P'Cola was sporting the biggest rock that he had ever seen on his huge finger. And the well-cut, tailored Armani suit he had on had to cost about two grand.

The two girls were shocked by P'Cola's unnecessary foul language. They were even more shocked after they saw Devontae and Keith away. Jamell, the one Keith was dancing with, smiled embarrassingly, then walked away. Her friend happily went on to the next man.

An open bottle of Moet chilled in a bucket of ice on the table next to two champagne glasses. The three of them sat down. P'Cola motioned for the waitress to bring another glass for him. When she returned, they poured drinks and sipped on the bubbly to loosen them up.

Keith jumped up when heard Usher's "No Limit" come on. All the ladies in the house sat down their drinks and rushed the dance floor.

P'Cola left Devontae and danced his way over to the DJ booth. He whispered into DJ Hurricane's ear, then reached into his pockets and took out a hundred dollar bill. He rolled it up and slid it to him.

***

There wasn't a parking spot left by the time Kylie and Misty pulled up outside. Kylie drove until she found a spot on the sidewalk. Both of them went into their purses, pulling out compact makeup kits. Satisfied with their looks, they got out the car, strutting across the street to the entrance. They both wore dresses with their lower backs out and three-inch heels.

As soon as they entered the club, they heard Tupac's "California Love" blasting through the speakers. Misty looked toward the DJ booth and saw P'Cola pointing at her. Impressed, she motioned for him to come over. He rushed over to her, greeting with a big hug.

"Ass kisser," she said jokingly. "But that was sweet."

"You liked that, huh?"

"Yeah. That was cool." She grabbed his hand, leading him to the dance floor. "Let's do this."

Keith unburied his face from Jamell's chest. He had bought her a few drinks to apologize for walking off on her earlier. If he had come up for air a second sooner, he would have seen Misty and P'Cola walk past him.

"I need a drink, baby," he said, pushing himself away from her.

She grabbed hold of his arm. "Tell me what you're drinking, and I'll get it for you," she insisted.

He snatched away from her death grip. "I'm cool," he said, checking to make sure he hadn't lost a cuff link. "I'm a catch up with you later."

"Don't forget," she yelled at his back while she watched his tight little ass as he walked away.

Keith was only two feet away from the bar when Kylie appeared out of nowhere. Her green eyes sparkled in the dimly lit place. She stood there smiling at him, looking better than he'd ever seen her.

"Can I dance with you, playa?" she asked, eyeing him up and down coolly. "You know you're the finest nigga in here, right?"

Ignoring her, he glanced around the club. He knew if Kylie was there, then so was Misty. P'Cola had done exactly what he'd expected. What he didn't expect was for Kylie to be there. He liked Kylie, but Misty just happened to have his full attention at the moment.

Giving up his eye search for Misty, he focused on Kylie. "Baby, when did you get here" He reached out and gave her a hug. The sweet fragrance of his cologne filled her nostrils, making her not want to let him go.

"A little while ago," she said. "I'm with Misty."

"Misty, Misty," he said softly, acting like he couldn't remember who she was.

"You remember her. The cute girl with the chinky eyes and the doll face," she said, describing her for him. "Don't stand there acting like you don't know who I'm talking about."

"Aw, yeah, yeah. Now I remember. The girl with the long hair, right?"

"Mm hm. Come on, let's go take some pictures." She took his hand. "You are looking too good in that suit."

He pulled her back. "Let's get a drink first. I'll follow you."

Keith lagged behind, getting a good look at her butt cheeks trying to bust out of her dress. She glanced back over her shoulder, catching him staring at her. That made her start switching her butt even harder.

Man, it's gonna break her heart after I fuck her friend, Keith thought. It's a damn shame I've got to be such a scandalous-ass nigga. Maybe in time, they'll learn to accept me fucking around with them both.

Kylie gazed at the rows of alcohol behind the bar. Out of the corner of her eye, she could see Keith staring her up and down. She was glad that his eyes were on her, because there was plenty of competition up in there. As good as Keith looked in his suit, he could've had any broad there.

A medium-sized athletically built brown-skinned dude, wearing a suit and a Atlanta Braves cap, told the bartender to get everybody at the bar a round, on him. The bartender went from person to person, with a rag draped over his shoulder, fixing people's drinks.

142

"Can I get you something, sweetie?" the bartender asked Kylie flirtatiously. He fixed his eyes on her partly-exposed breasts. "Don't worry, it's on the big time Braves player standing at the end of the bar."

"Just a minute," she said to him, then turned to Keith. "Let's see. I bet you want some Moet, right?"

"You know how I like it."

She smiled, turning back to the bartender. "Get us two glasses of Mo, please."

"Make it a bottle," Keith said. "I can pay for my own drinks." The bartender shrugged and did as he was told.

P'Cola was on the dance floor, two stepping with Misty. He stepped back away from her as he spun her around. While doing so, she caught a glimpse of Keith standing at the bar, playing in Kylie's hair. The overcrowded dance floor was getting hot, causing sweat droplets to appear on Misty's forehead. She quit dancing.

"It's a little hot in here," she said fanning herself. "Come on, you can buy me a drink." She pulled him over to the bar where Kylie and Keith were conversing.

P'Cola saw Keith and threw his arm around Misty's shoulders. A mischievous grin appeared on his face. He stopped at the bar pretending that he didn't see Keith standing there.

Keith's back was turned to them when Misty stepped up to the bar, accidentally bumping into him. Quickly, he cut his conversation short with Kylie and turned around to the beautiful sight that stood between him and P'Cola.

"Excuse me," she said in a sexy, low voice. "I didn't mess up your suit, did I?"

He had temporarily gone into a daze again. For some strange reason, the very sight of her always left him speechless.

He collected himself. "It's cool." He could see P'Cola standing over her grinning from ear to ear. "I see you're in here with the finest woman in the house tonight."

Misty blushed. "Thank you, Kei--"

"What you mean, she the finest woman in the house?" Kylie snapped. "What about me?"

He turned to Kylie. "I'm just doing a little light-weight flirting, that's all baby." He kissed her on the forehead. "Just be cool and finish your drink."

She put her hand on her hip, looking up at him. "Don't talk to me like I'm a goddamn child, Keith," she said hotly. She guzzled down the rest of her drink, then set the glass on the bar. "I have to go to the....ladies room," she said drunkenly. "Misty, you comin'?"

Misty took her eyes off Keith and focused in on Kylie. "Naw, I think I'ma hang out here with the boys."

Kylie spun on her heels, marching toward the restroom. "Fuckin' whore!" she said to herself.

P'Cola tried to use Kylie to get rid of Keith. "You'd better go make up with your girl," he said, nodding in her direction.

Keith brushed her off. "She'll be alright." He looked Misty dead in her face. "You know how women get when another beautiful woman is in their presence."

She took that as a compliment and ran with it. "I'm glad I don't have that problem."

"I bet you don't." He picked up the bottle of Moet off the bar. "Let me pour you a drink." He poured the champagne into Kylie's empty glass, then handed it to Misty.

"Thanks. You're a real gentleman," she complimented him.

"Ain't he?" P'Cola said sarcastically. "It's too bad he doesn't know how to be a gentleman with his own girl."

Misty suppressed a smile. The thought of two friends falling out over her created moisture between her legs. A little competition was just what P'Cola needed to loosen his pockets for a little more. She could already feel the down-payment money for her new car in the palm of her hand. Though she already had more than enough to get one herself, she would never pass up the chance to spend someone else's money.

Nearly drunk, Keith sipped on his drink while staring at P'Cola through red eyes. "You know a playa like me ain't got to be a gentleman all the time, P'Cola. Only when I'm on a mission."

Misty couldn't help but ask. "What kind of a mission are you on now?"

He swallowed the remainder of his drink. "Taking somebody's woman." He smacked his lips.

P'Cola smiled nastily. If he responded to that comment, he would look like a hater in front of Misty. If he didn't respond to it, he would feel like a straight up chump. He was in a no win situation, so fuck it. Why not get in his ass?

P'Cola stepped his huge frame around Misty, getting up in Keith's face. "What kinda shit you on tonight?" he said angrily.

Keith sat the bottle of Moet on top of the bar. "You said she was free game, nigga," he reminded P'Cola. "Don't start hating now 'cause I'm trying to make a move."

P'Cola tried to calm down. "I don't even know why I'm tripping'. Ain't like you can take a bitch from me no way."

A frown appeared on Keith's face. He didn't really think he could whoop P'Cola, but the Moet was kicking in like courage juice. Plus, he had his strap out in the car.

"Why don't you let the lady choose, fat boy," Keith suggested.

That was it. P'Cola grabbed Keith by the neck with one hand and picked up a bottle of Moet with the other. He was about to smack Keith upside the head with it until Devontae appeared out of nowhere.

"P'Cola, what's up, man?" Devontae asked.

"Ain't nothin' up with that nigga and me no more," P'Cola replied.

"I don't give a fuck!" Keith said. "You ain't shit but a hater anyway." P'Cola ignored him and started walking away with Misty in tow. "Nigga, from now on you better keep every bitch you got away from me." he yelled, walking after him. He told the bartender to send the bill to his table. He paid no attention to the staring crowd as he walked back to VIP.

Devontae walked quickly, trying to keep up. "What the fuck was that shit all about?"

Keith ignored him until he got to the table. He sat down and poured himself another drink. He swallowed it, poured another glass, then did the same.

Devontae waited on him to finish before he said, "You gon' tell me what all that was about? I leave you alone for a few minutes and you almost get your ass kicked."

"That was a face out," Keith said. "A tactic that I had to use in order to get wit' that ho. You know what I'm saying?"

"No!"

"It's simple. She won't fuck with me if she thinks what we're cool. With us being into it, it gives her a chance to work both sides to her advantage. After I fuck her, I'll apologize to him.

"What about Kylie?" Devontae quizzed. "Ain't they best friends?"

"I'm about to handle that right now." He could see Kylie looking around the club for him. She had been inside the restroom the whole time, and didn't have a clue what was going on.

Keith leaned toward Devontae. "I need you to call Natalie. Tell her that you want her to come up here and kick it with us."

Devontae smiled, finally realizing what Keith's plan was. "Aw, I see what you're up to. Now you're about to fall out with Kylie, too?"

"Don't try to figure me out. Just make the call."

"Why are you so obsessed with that bitch, man?"

Keith said, "To be honest, that bitch is poison. I know she is. He rubbed his hand across his face in bewilderment. "But I got to have her." He couldn't believe that those words escaped from his lips.

Devontae pulled out his cell phone and dialed Natalie's number. Keith snatched the phone out of his hand.

"Don't do it here. Go to the restroom. I'm about to call Kylie over here. I want to be in the VIP tricking with her when Natalie walks in the door."

"Ain't you worried about getting into it with Natalie? You can't risk your whole stable over one ho."

Keith brushed him off. "Just do what I told you to do. Then take a seat at the bar and watch a playa work."

Devontae stood up. "A'ight, playa." He started to walk off, then turned back around. "I hope this bitch is worth it. That ho better be worth ten hoes."

"Man, just go." He waited until Devontae left before he stood up, getting Kylie's attention, then called her over.

Once they got outside, Misty began to pull away with P'Cola. She had almost forgotten about Kylie. There was no way she was gonna get up and leave without letting her know first.

"Wait, P'Cola!" she exclaimed. "I gotta go back in there and tell Kylie that I'm leaving."

He looked down at her with his nose wrinkled up. "Fuck Kylie! She'll figure it out."

"Unt unh." I'm not gon' just leave her like that," she said. "Just because you and yo' boy are into it don't mean we are."

She tried to go back inside but he grabbed her. "Find Kylie and tell her what you got to say and come the fuck outta there," he commanded. "Don't say one word to that sucka. I'm through fuckin' with him."

"Damn, P'Cola, he was just messing with you," she said, trying to cheer him up.

"Just do what I told you to do."

"Okay, baby," she said humbly. "Be right back." She jogged lightly in her heels back into the club.

Kylie was giggling from the wet tongue that Keith stuck in her ear. She had gotten a little tipsy and was ready to fuck. He stopped briefly to wet his lips with champagne then continued to tongue fuck her ear. Slowly, he eased his hand in between their bodies and began to play with her breasts.

She closed her eyes, feeling a tingling sensation between her legs. She reached the point where she didn't care who was around or watching.

"I want to fuck you," he whispered into her ear. His warm breath tickled the sensitive hairs inside her ear, causing her to squirm in her seat. "Would you fuck me right here if I asked you to?"

"Yess."

"Ump umm," Misty grunted, interrupting them.

They both looked up in a hurry and saw Misty standing over them. "I don't mean to interrupt you two freaks, but I didn't want to leave without telling you first, Kylie."

Kylie had a frustrated look on her face. She had reached the point where she didn't want Misty around while she was with Keith. He had already told her that Misty had left with P'Cola.

She forced a smile. "Okay, I'ma stay and kick it with him for a while. You have your key?"

Misty was looking at Keith. For a moment, she thought she was looking at KC, sitting there all hugged up with another girl. Somehow, she was gonna find a reason to be alone with him. She wanted to find out what he was like mentally and sexually.

"Misty!" Kylie yelled, getting her attention.

She snapped out of it. "Huh?"

"I asked you if you had your key."

"Yeah, I got it. I'll see you when you get home." She glanced at Keith one last time. "I'll see you later."

Verbally, he didn't respond, he just raised his glass at her. She didn't say it, but he could tell that he had an open invitation to get at her. He gave her a knowing wink before she turned to leave.

P'Cola looked into the mirror after he heard music coming from the car that pulled up behind his truck. A familiar-looking face hopped out of a Red Nissan Armada. She was petite and wore micro braids pinned up at the back. He searched his memory bank as he watched her strut toward the club. She was looking sexy in a pair of suede boots that came up to her knees and a loose fitting skirt.

He snapped his fingers, finally remembering who he was. "That's where I know her from," he said to himself. "That's Keith's little broad, Natalie."

148

While Natalie was entering the club, Misty was exiting. Natalie got a good look at the gorgeous woman as they passed each other. She would have bet her last dollar that Keith had her number in his phone or had bought her plenty of drinks trying to get it. Knowing him, she was probably old news. With all of his cheating and neglect, Natalie often wondered why she still loved him.

"Hi," Natalie said, speaking to Misty, who almost bumped into her. Misty, being snotty, ignored her and kept on walking. On a normal night, Misty would have copped an attitude and tried to fight her. But at the moment, all she wanted to do was sit across from Keith and have a few drinks.

Entering the club, she heard "Beyonce's "Diva" bumping through the speakers. Devontae eased up behind her.

"Buy a drink?'

Her frown turned into a smile when she turned around and saw Devontae's yellow face.

"Hey, boy. I thought you were one of these fools." She gave him a hug. "Where is my man at?"

He nodded toward Keith's table. The frown returned after she saw Keith freaking the shit out of Kylie in the VIP. She bit down on her bottom lip.

"That's why I called you over here tonight," Devontae said. "You see that shit right there? I'd kick his ass if I was you."

She handed Devontae her purse and stormed across the room to his table. Keith dipped Kylie's fingers into his glass and was sucking the champagne off them. The loud sounds of Natalie's boots hitting the hard floor made him turn to look. But it was too late. Natalie punched him in the eye.

"Shoot!" he hollered, grabbing his face. It took a minute for him to figure out what was going on.

He felt the cut under his eye. Before he could get up, Natalie grabbed the empty Moet bottle, drew back and busted him upside his head with it. Kylie watched in horror. Devontae saw what was happening and took off in their direction.

The bottle didn't break. Kylie tried to escape, but not before Natalie struck her across her back with the fat end of the bottle. She fell to the ground, holding her back, screaming out in pain.

Devontae finally made it over to where they were. Natalie raised the bottle again, but before she could swing, she felt Devontae's hand wrap around her neck. He took the bottle away from her. She kicked and clawed until he pushed her down. Soon the bouncer stepped in and assisted him.

Keith was on the floor, holding his head in a daze. He wasn't sure where he was or what had happened. The crowd was hyped and circled the area, screaming for the bouncer to let Natalie go. Cuffing her hands behind her back, they immediately escorted her out of the club.

Devontae helped his friend up off the floor. By then the police and paramedics had come running into the club, clearing away the crowd.

Keith saw them putting Kylie on the stretcher. "What the fuck happened?" he said groggily.

"Shit got out of hand, playa," Devontae said, shaking his head.

CHAPTER EIGHTEEN

The next morning, Keith sat in his office popping pain pills and drinking coffee. He wouldn't have shown up for work, but he had used up all of his sick days and couldn't afford to lose his job right now. His commission, plus the scam he had going, brought in about ten grand a month, easily. The only other way he could've made that kind of money was by selling dope. That or luck up on a corporate job, which he knew wasn't happening.

Subconsciously he fiddled with the bandage that was wrapped around his head. Before he left the hospital last night, he stopped and made sure that Kylie was gonna be alright. The doctors informed him that she would be fine. Natalie didn't swing the bottle hard enough to break any bones, but her back and shoulders were bruised badly.

"Natalie, Natalie, Natalie," he repeated to himself.

He always thought of her as his ghetto girl, and last night she proved it. He still couldn't believe that she could've killed me? he thought to himself. Did she even care? As much as he didn't want to, he had to cut her off completely. Any girl who had the guts to do that to him, he didn't need. If he ever saw her again, she had an ass whooping coming.

Keith sat back in his chair, looking out of his huge window. An attractive white lady and a teenaged boy were looking at a Dodge Challenger. He saw the owner conversing with two stuck-up looking white guys in cheap suits. He closed his eyes, trying to forget about the pain in his head.

"Knock, knock," a female voice said.

His eyes opened slowly. Misty was standing in the doorway looking fine as a muthafucka.

He sat up in his chair, wondering what it was that brought her there. For a minute, he was speechless, like he always was at the sight of her. He didn't know why, but this girl brought butterflies to his stomach.

She stepped into his office. "You do remember me?" she asked.

He smiled. "I'd have to lose all the brain cells in my head to forget something as fine as you," he said coolly, trying to collect himself. "Have a seat."

Misty sat in one of the two leather chairs and crossed her legs. "I was out car shopping, so I decided to stop in and see how you were doing."

"How'd you find out where I worked?" he quizzed.

With a shrug, she said, "You know all car dealers put their names on the back of every car they sell. I got yours off of Kylie's."

"She knows you're here?"

She shook her head. "You know better than that." Her eyes remained on him. "So, how ya feeling?"

He touched his bandage lightly. "I'm cool. How's Kylie?"

"Banged the fuck up," she said, then set her purse on his desk.

They stared at each other lustfully. Neither said a word.

Keith cleared his throat. "Why don't we get down to what you really came for," he said, hoping that she was gonna come on to him.

She knew what he wanted her to say, and she wanted to say it, but she also wanted to make him sweat a little.

Uncrossing her legs, she said, "Okay. I really came to...check out that F-150 out there." She smiled for a minute. "You think my credit is good enough?"

Evidently, she knew about the long program that he had going.

Resting his elbows on the armrests, he interlocked his fingers and said, "If it's credit that you're looking for, you've come to the right place."

Standing up, she placed a finger on his desk and slowly walked around it to where he was sitting. He turned toward her. "Why don't you run a check on me right now?" she said seductively.

The only button that was fastened on her ping button-down shirt was the middle one. Part of her breasts, as well as her navel ring, were exposed.

152

"First we ha--" She bent over and kissed him with her eyes closed.

"Mmm," he moaned, tasting her sweet saliva. She took her tongue out of his mouth and guided his face into her chest. He had forgotten about the pain in his head altogether.

"Be gentle, baby," she murmured, feeling his teeth biting down on her left nipple. "Yeess."

Suddenly, she backed away from him, stopping everything. He sat there with his chest heaving, staring up at her. Buttoning her shirt, she walked back to the other side of his desk.

"We through?"

"For now," she said evenly. "I came here to buy a new car. Not to fuck."

He rubbed his hand over his face, laughing to himself. "That's cold."

"Ain't it?" She reached into her purse and pulled out a bundle of money, tossing it on his desk. "That's ten grand. I've been preapproved for an eighteen-thousand-dollar loan from New Horizon Federal Credit Union, co-signed by Paris Coleman, aka P'Cola." She gave him a wicked little smile. "So, I won't be needing a loan from you."

Once again, he was left speechless. This girl had a lot of games.

"What's the matter?" she asked. "Cat got your tongue?"

He looked down at her crotch. A wide V-shape bulged out the front of her pants. "No yet," he replied.

She caught the remark after she saw what his eyes were focused on. "This kitty cat ain't no stray. So I should warn you that it's very high maintenance." She sat down and crossed her legs so he wouldn't be distracted. "Now, could we start the paperwork on my new truck, please?"

"A'ight," he said, opening his desk drawer. "But one of these days, we're gonna finish what we started."

"You definitely got that coming. But, you can't kiss and tell."

"I'm a playa, baby. Not a hater."

"We'll see."

***

"So you coming or what?" Fabien asked. "I don't have time for games. I think you fakin'."

"I told you that I was coming," Stacy whispered into the phone. She was in the bathroom, pretending to be peeing while P'Cola was in the bedroom, getting dressed to go out. "As soon as he leaves, I'll be on my way."

Fabien was sitting on the edge of his bed, oiling up his muscular frame. "Aight. I'll be waiting."

"I hope you got some protection, 'cause I ain't trying to get---" P'Cola walked through the door. "Okay, girl, I'll see you Monday," she said, pretending to be talking to one of her girlfriends. "Bye." She hung up.

"What the hell is Amber talkin' bout now?" he asked.

"How do you know that I was talking to her?" She wiped herself, pulled up her shorts and flushed the toilet.

P'Cola grunted. "That's the only friend you got besides me. Yo' attitude is too bad."

That's what you think, she thought to herself. That was your boy on the phone, begging me to come over. And I'm gonna fuck him tonight. She held back a smile while she stood beside him, washing her hands in the sink. If he only knew what I was thinking, he would slap my ass through the wall.

P'Cola left the house about an hour later. Stacy could tell that he was going to meet Misty by how anxious he was. She gave a fuck, but then gain, she didn't. She was going to lay up with a hard body tonight, and that was all she could think about at the moment. At first she was out for revenge, but after the three wonderful dates that she and Fabien had been on, she started to develop feelings for him.

After a quick shower with her favorite shower gel, she slipped into a colorful sundress and a pair of sandals. No underwear would be needed for what she was going to do. She was trying to get fucked tonight. She made Fabien wait long enough. She looked in the mirror one last time, blew herself a kiss, then grabbed her keys and headed out the door.

A warm breeze was coming in from the South. Taking advantage of the wonderful weather. Stacy hit the button that dropped the top of her Mustang. She popped in Rihanna's "Diamonds," then took off down the road.

Stacy cut her lights out before she pulled into Fabien's driveway. He lived in an all white neighborhood in West Mobile. he warned her before she got there that his nosey white neighbors be tripping about him having company pull up at all hours of the night.

Raising the top to her car, she checked her face in the mirror and walked up to the front door. Fabien answered the door wearing house shoes, red pajama bottoms and a tank top. Without a word, she put her arms around him and began kissing his lips and face. He backed up so he could close the door. Stacy continued to kiss him savagely, pushing him back against the wall. He relaxed, letting her take control. Roughly she licked and bit his chest, then dropped to her knees, tonguing his navel while pulling down his pajamas. He put his hand on top of her head, pushing it down to his dick. Most of it fit into her mouth on the first try. She took it out, swallowed, then forced it down her throat, sucking it and wiggling her tongue around inside her mouth.

Fabien closed his eyes while she did her thing. He felt kind of bad for what he was doing behind P'Cola's back, but he did nothing to stop it.

P'Cola and Misty were riding in her new F-150 on the way to the show. She sat on the passenger side, twisting up a blunt while he sipped on a glass of Remy Martin. V.S.O.P. He felt his cell phone vibrating on his hip.

"Hello," he answered.

"P'Cola, this is Wayne, man. I'm trying to get three of them thangs, like right now."

"Damn! Me and my lady friend are on our way to the show. You can't wait?"

"Not really, man. It's kinda poppin' down my way and I wanna get it while the gettin' is good," Wayne explained.

P'Cola thought for a moment. He had never revealed to Misty that his real income came from slanging bricks of cocaine. If he made the move with her in the truck, she would probably put two and two together. He didn't need that. It was bad enough that Stacy knew all of his business. That's why he was scared to exchange her for Misty.

If he didn't drop everything and go meet Wayne, he was gonna miss out on fifty-seven grand, and that he wasn't about to do. He would be just as discreet as he could while he handled his business.

"A'ight," P'Cola finally said. "Meet me at my house on Clay Street in about..." he glanced at his watch, "fifteen minutes."

"Don't be bullshittin', P'Cola, man. I know how you are."

"Fifteen minutes." He hung up.

P'Cola made a left, passed the median, then made another left, heading back north on St. Stephens Road. A confused look appeared on Misty's face when she noticed that they were going in the opposite direction.

"Where we goin?" she inquired.

"I gotta make a quick run."

She frowned. "But the show starts in twenty minutes!" she exclaimed.

"We're gonna make it, baby. Just calm down."

She became suspicious. The closer she got to P'Cola, the more she noticed that he made sudden moves, like a nigga who had the sack. But she never saw any physical proof that he fucked around, except for the ten grand cash that he gave her to put down on her new truck.

Wayne was parked outside the house on Clay Street in his white Suburban. He waited impatiently for P'Cola to show up. All of a sudden a red F-150 came flying over the hill and whipped into the driveway. Wayne didn't move until he saw P'Cola's big head after the interior late came on.

"Be right back," P'Cola said on his way out the truck.

This was the first time that Misty had heard about P'Cola having another house. She could've moved in there a long time ago and never had to deal with Stacy's shit. She reminded herself to talk to P'Cola about that after he finished taking care of his business.

Wayne stepped out of the Suburban, wearing sweatpants and a tank top. He held a black gym bag in his hand.

"Wha'sup, baby?" Wayne said, giving P'Cola a handshake.

"Shit. Let's hurry up and do this." P'Cola unlocked the door and they both went inside.

Inside the house, Wayne was told to wait in the living room while P'Cola ran upstairs to the attic. Tucked away in a corner was a large trunk with an old Master Lock securing it. Opening it up, he took out three kilos, then locked it back up.

Wayne was bent over, looking at a big goldfish trying to get away from two killer piranhas inside the fish tank. He glanced up after he heard P'Cola coming down the steps.

"Everything straight?"

"Yep." P'Cola set the dope on the dining room table. "Come on back here."

"Who in the car wit' you?" Wayne asked as he set his bag down on the table.

P'Cola smiled proudly. "I got a bad one in the car," he bragged. "Stop and take a look at her on your way to your truck."

"Man, I...I...ain...ain't fittna be...doing all that." Wayne stuttered when he became excited.

"Hatin'a get you nowhere." P'Cola grabbed the gym bag. "Is this my money?"

Wayne looked up from checking out the dope. "Um...ye...yeah. But...buut, I'ma need my bag back."

P'Cola emptied the stacks of money onto the table, then tossed him the bag. It wasn't until after Wayne was gone that he put up the money.

***

Leaning back in the seat, smoking on the blunt that she had rolled earlier, Misty waited impatiently for P'Cola to return. She saw Wayne come out of the house, moving quickly, with the black bag in his hand. He even looked like he was doing something illegal. She made a mental note to remember where the house was. The episode was enough for her to want to start investigating P'Cola's background. If he was fucking with dope, he was gonna have to start kicking in more than he was.

When it was halfway gone, she put the blunt out so P'Cola could get his buzz on, too. A few minutes later, he climbed his big body into the truck.

"You ready, baby?" He took a sip of his now watery drink. "Where the blunt at?"

She took it out of the ashtray and handed it to him. Her eyes watched him closely as he inhaled the smoke into his lungs. He saw her watching him, but he avoided all eye contact.

"P'Cola?"

"Huh?"

"What did you just do? If you don't mind me asking."

He hesitated for a minute, searching for a good lie to tell her. A suitable one didn't come to mind quickly. What else could he have been doing, meeting Wayne at a secret place, taking time out of their date, if he weren't dealing drugs? Then Wayne came and went, carrying a black gym bag. A seven-year-old could've figured out what they were up to.

His silence confirmed her suspicions. Even though she knew that he was in the right by keeping his business secret, she was still a little hurt. She thought she had his nose open wide enough that he would keep no secrets from her.

"You sellin' dope, P'Cola," she blurted out. "I wondered how you gave me that ten grand so easily." She wanted him to go ahead and confess.

Blowing smoke out of his nostrils, he threw the rest of the blunt out of the window. "I don't know if you forgot or not, but I am a business owner."

She smirked. "Not gonna confess, huh?"

He lifted his shoulders. "Ain't nothin' to confess."

Her attention went to a white kid who was standing up in the back seat of the car next to them. If that's how he wanted to play it, she would leave it at that for the time being.

***

Slim Vegas and KC had their heads buried deep inside two old, thick and confusing law books. Weeks had gone by and they still hadn't found anything useful. Several times, KC became frustrated and wanted to give up, but Slim Vegas wasn't trying to hear it. He didn't want KC to spend his young life locked up. If he could help set him free, he would feel better about his chances of winning his own appeal.

"Hand me your case, KC," Slim Vegas said, closing the law book. "I'ma take it back to the cell and go through it again."

KC eagerly tossed him the small stack of papers. "Good luck, man." He lowered his head down onto the table.

Getting up out of his chair, Slim Vegas stretched his old bones, then walked over to the door and beat on it, "CO," he called out. "I'm ready to go back to my cell." He looked down at KC. "Keep ya head up, young bro. Everything is gonna be alright."

KC didn't respond, nor did he lift his head. He wasn't gonna go home for ten years. All of this law library shit was a waste of time, he thought. What he should've been doing was writing some of his old hoes so he could start getting visits. His mother kept his books straight, so he was cool with money. Female companionship was what he needed.

That night he stayed up late, writing letters to every heavy set girl he knew out in the world. It wasn't no use trying to get in touch with the fine ones. A nigga in jail was of no use to them. There were too many ballers out there who kept them on lock. Big girls paid like they weighed.

Slim Vegas had his shirt off, exposing his hairy, graying back, reading KC's case. Young people these days are so stupid, he thought. He wouldn't believe that KC would rather sit on his bunk, writing letters, than work on his own case. Unknown to KC, Slim Vegas wasn't working for free. If he did happen to luck up and beat his case, KC would owe him dearly.

Slim Vegas had a daughter behind who needed financial help out in the free world. If everything worked out, KC would be the one who would help her.

Hours went by, KC had fallen asleep a long time ago, but Slim Vegas was still at work. Yawning, he took off his glasses, then set them down on the bed.

"Shit!" he said to himself. He had gone over every single page, coming up with nothing.

He was just about to give up for the night, when a thought entered his mind. He didn't remember seeing KC's signature on his Miranda form. Just to be sure, he looked over the document once more. Just like he thought, KC's signature was nowhere on the form.

Instantly, he jumped up off the bed. "KC, get up!" he yelled, shaking him awake.

"Whaat?" KC mumbled, smacking his dry lips. "Man, I just went to sleep. You need to take yo' ass to bed." he rolled over, facing the wall. "Put that shit up."

"Do you remember signing a Miranda form before you made your statement?"

Knowing that Slim Vegas wasn't gonna let it go, he sat up, wiping the sleep from his eyes. "What?

Slim Vegas spoke slowly. "Do you remember signing away your Miranda rights?

"Miranda? Nah, I didn't sign anything. They just pulled out a tape recorder and I started talking. All I was trying to do was make sure Misty didn't go down with me."

A triumphant smile appeared on Slim Vegas's face. "I think we have a chance to get you out of here, young bro. At least out on an appeal bond."

"The judge said he didn't give bonds on murder cases."

"He didn't because of the statement you made during your interrogation. I read it in your report. Without your signature on this form" he held it up at him, "it's like you never confessed."

"You bullshittin'?"

"No, I'm not." He snatched the covers off of KC. "Get up! We've got a motion to prepare!"

Von Diesel

CHAPTER NINETEEN

Empire was showing on the big screen television in the living room of Misty's now home. She had finally sucked P'Cola's dick and told him that she wanted to be his wifey. Of course, she was only bullshitting. As a result, he bought her a small house near the airport, far away from his home with Stacy.

P'Cola had driven his RV out to Panama City for the week, no doubt going to get some more drugs. Kylie was still in a lot of pain and didn't want to hang out. That left Misty lonely when she wasn't running the shop.

She sat on her couch in front of the TV with her arms and legs crossed, shaking her foot nervously. "I'm not gonna sit here by myself tonight," she said to herself.

Digging into her purse, she searched until she found Keith's business card. She picked up the phone and called his home number. Now she too had butterflies in her stomach while she waited for him to pick up.

Keith stood over his stove, frying chicken. He had the phone up to his ear, talking to Robin, when he heard the line click.

"Robin asked, "So what time is dinner gonna be ready?"

"Hold on right quick. My line is clicking." He clicked over. "Hello."

"You on the phone?" Misty asked in a sexy voice.

Smiling, he said, "Yep, but it ain't nobody special."

Misty picked up the remote, turning the volume down on the TV. "Hang her up, then."

"Hold on a minute." He clicked back over. "Robin, let me call you back in a little while, okay, baby?"

She sighed. "Aw, man!" she pouted. "Why come I can't never get no quality time? Here we are planning a dinner date, and then you get a call. Now, all of a sudden you gonna call me back. Fuck that shit man!"

"Robin, don't--" he stopped in mid-sentence after he heard Misty hang up on the other end.

Robin heard it as well. "The bitch hung up."

"What are you talking about? What bitch?"

The line clicked again. "Hold on." He clicked over. "Hello."

"You left me on hold," Misty reminded him.

He turned the stove off. "I didn't mean to," he explained. "I had a little problem on the other line."

With her feet propped up on the glass coffee table, Misty fiddled with her belly ring. "It's cool. Now you gotta leave her on hold like you did me."

"So, to what do I owe the pleasure?" He drained the chicken grease into its proper container.

"I've been thinking about you."

"Good or bad?"

"Mmm, a little of both." She slid her hand down under her pajamas and began rubbing her bald pussy. The sound of his soothing voice turned her on. "What you got on, baby?"

Robin finally hung up. He looked down at his legs. "Right now, I have on a pair of Polo briefs and some house shoes. And you?"

"I got on some Misty's secret."

He grabbed his dick. "How can I find out what the secret is?"

"Grab a six pack of Coronas and something to smoke on, then head this way."

"I heard he bought you a house."

"And?"

"And, you're inviting me over there?'

"Like you said, he bought me a house, and I'm inviting you to come over and kick it with me."

He shook his head. "Girl, you playin' a dirty game."

"That's because I'm a dirty girl. He's out of town anyway. Now bring your scary ass over here and fuc--see me, boy."

He laughed after he heard what she almost let slip. After he wrote down her address, they hung up. The chicken went into the trash can instead of his stomach. He now had a yen for some cat. It was dick that she had called for in the first place. He didn't know what took her so long to ask for it.

The first thing he did was hop into the shower. One thing that turned a woman on was a man who smelled good. When he finished, he lotioned his body, making sure that his feet and knees were just as smooth as his face. The Dax wave grease made his hair wave like an ocean current. He put on a fresh T-shirt, jogging shorts and a pair of Nike flip-flops. He didn't want to dress up just to go over there and get undressed.

Before he left, he took his gun out of the top drawer, putting it inside his pocket. Going to see a woman over to her man's house could be dangerous. Whether P'Cola bought it for her or not, it was still his in a sense. So he wasn't gonna go alone.

In the bathroom, he checked his face in the mirror one last time. Damn, he thought as he looked at his reflection. That knot Natalie put on my head is still there. He cut out the light and shut the door.

The phone rang as he was walking by. He looked at it, wondering if should answer it or let the machine pick up. It rang again. This time he answered it, just in case it was Misty calling back.

"Hello," he answered. There was silence. "Hello."

"Hi," a familiar female voice said. "Member me?"

"Yes. How you doing, Kylie?" He closed his eyes. He didn't have time to patch things up with her right now, or ever.

"I'm fine. She sounded so sweet and innocent. "I'm barely walking, but I should be alright in a few weeks." She paused. "Look Keith, we've got some things that we need to discuss."

"I don't mean to be rude, but I'm in kind of a hurry."

Don't mean to be rude? thought Kylie. I can't believe what this nigga just said. I get my ass kicked because of him and don't get so much as an apology? But he don't mean to be rude. I don't know why I bothered. I should've taken his absence as a hint.

"Okay," Kylie said sheepishly. "I'll just call you some other time."

"Cool. Talk to you later."

Kylie slammed the phone down. She got up off the couch, limping to her bedroom. Her body collapsed onto her bed. She squeezed her pillow tight and started to cry.

After Misty hung up the phone with Keith, she hopped into the shower as well. She was excited about seeing him and couldn't wait to feel his body next to hers. Deep down, she wanted him just as bad as he wanted her, but she was gonna take her time with him. If he turned out to be the nigga she thought he was, KC might not ever see her again.

She lotioned her body with her favorite scent---cucumber melon. She loved how good it smelled and hoped that he would too. She was ready by the time she heard Keith's Camaro pull into her driveway. Her toenails were polished, her nails were done and her hair was pulled back into a wavy ponytail, making her eyes even more slanted than they were already.

He rang the doorbell.

She hurried toward the door, then stopped about three feet away from it to calm herself down.

"Hi," she said, after she opened the door.

The first thing he noticed was her pretty bare feet. His eyes wandered up her long, smooth legs to the oversized T-shirt that hung down to her thighs.

"You look good," he complimented her. He handed over the six-pack of Coronas. "Can I come in, or is that all you wanted?"

"I'm sorry." She had a few nasty thoughts of her own, looking down at the crotch of his shorts. "Come in."

Not only was the outside of the house nice, but P'Cola had furnished the whole interior with expensive furniture and appliances. Keith wondered how in the hell he afforded it all.

He made himself comfortable on the sofa while she took the beer to the kitchen. To his surprise, she had the old movie "The Mach" playing on the screen.

"You're a Goldie fan, huh?" he yelled toward the kitchen.

"She came back into the living room carrying two open bottles of Corona. "Yep. If I would've been the same age that I am now, back in the seventies, I would've been his main whore."

He laughed. "Damn." He took a beer from her. "Not his main ho."

"I stay down for my man and whatever he does," she stated firmly. "Did you bring the greens?"

"Aw, yeah." He pulled out a quarter ounce of light greens. "I forgot to get the blunts."

"That's okay. I got some in the back."

His eyes were fixed on her booty as she walked down the hallway. Man, he couldn't wait to hit that. P'Cola was probably hitting it good, but his stomach was too big for him to really get up in it. She looked pretty flexible herself. He grinned, unable to hold back his excitement. As big of a player as he was, he couldn't believe how he was reacting over one broad.

When she returned, he noticed that she had changed clothes. Now she was wearing a tank top and a pair of silk shorts. Her nipples damn near pierced her top. He loved those small, perky titties.

She took a seat in a chair next to the sofa where he was sitting, then emptied the greens onto the table. She broke it down, sprinkled some into a zigzag, then twisted it up.

"You don't mind smoking papers, do you?" she asked. She left the blunts on her dresser because they would have made her too high, and she wanted to remain in control of herself.

"Paper's cool." He couldn't help but stare at her. It wasn't just her beauty and booty, her style attracted him as well.

"So, have you talked to Kylie?" She put the lotion between her lips, then set fire to it. "That's your girl, ain't it?"

He smiled shyly. "There you go."

"What you mean..." she coughed, "there I go?" She passed the joint to him.

Accepting it, he smoked on it for a minute or two. "You bringing up someone that I'm trying to forget." He sipped his beer. "I'm trying to get next to you."

Picking up her beer, she got up, walked over to the love seat, then dropped down next to him. She made sure that her leg touched his. Sitting back on the sofa, she faced him while he coolly puffed on the joint. The sight of his juicy lips, sucking,

167

made her wet. She wanted to get on top of him and ride him forever.

He could see her pretty browns gazing at him out of the corner of his eye. That's why he made sure that he looked extra cool, blowing the smoke out of his nostrils.

"You are so fine. You know that?" She gently touched the knot on his head. "That crazy-ass girl don't play about you." She chuckled. "You must have some fire-ass head."

He passed what was left of the joint to her. "You think that's funny?"

"Naw, boy. I was just teasing."

For half the night they sat, drank, smoked and talked about everything from sex to the goals they were trying to reach. Keith admitted that he was a player who manipulated women every time he got the chance. She told him that even though she was a female, she was down for her crown and would do anything for the scrilla.

Then KC's name came up. She admitted that most of her feelings for Keith were because they looked so much alike. Keith's face had attracted her at first sight. Then, just to score some points, he told her that he staged the fight with P'Cola and the one between Natalie and Kylie just to get next to her.

Misty thought he was just as devious as she was. She sat Indian-style on the couch while he lay back on the armrest with his foot in her hand. Her soft hands massaged it while he shared his plans for their future. She wanted to be with him, but she was not about to jeopardize the good thing she already had going with P'Cola. At least not anytime soon.

Their conversation ran out. There was nothing left to discuss at four in the morning. By his calculations, he should have been in her panties two hours ago. She hadn't even hinted around that she wanted to have sex with him. If she didn't make a move within the next thirty minutes, he surely would.

All of a sudden she got up and disappeared into the back room. He sat up on the couch preparing for whatever was about to happen next. His eyes were on the TV, but he wasn't watching it."

Mint Conditions, *Pretty Brown Eyes* could be heard coming from her bedroom. "You gonna sit there all night or are you gonna come back here and keep me company?" she asked seductively.

Turning to face her, he saw that she had changed again. Nia Long could have walked into the room and wouldn't have diverted his attention away from her. With her hands touching both sides of the doorway, she stood there in a black lace and satin chemise with a matching thong.

He licked his lips as he got up to follow her into the bedroom. It was just as plush as the rest of the house. The whole bedroom set was mahogany and thick, walnut-colored carpet covered the entire floor. Her bed stood about three feet high with a small, two-step mahogany staircase next to it.

"Why don't you relax on the bed and make yourself comfortable?" she suggested. "I'll be back in a minute." She disappeared again.

Keith hurried out of his clothes, then neatly placed them on the seat of a mahogany rocking chair that sat in a corner of the room. Getting down on the floor, he did fifty push-ups to harden the muscles in his chest and arms.

The sheets felt cold and crisp, like she had just changed them before he showed up. He lay in the huge bed, pulling the comforter up to his waist, then waited for her to return.

Misty snuck off to the kitchen. Out of the cabinets, she got a jar of honey and a small bow. Emptying a third of the honey into the bowl, she let a little water from the faucet run into it to make it less sticky, then stirred it until it became creamy. She took off her chemise and thong. After scooping some of the concoction, she rubbed it all over her neck, titties, stomach, in between her thighs and even her feet. She slipped back into her chemise and headed back toward her bedroom. She wanted her body to taste naturally sweet when he kissed her.

Keith was sitting up in the bed with one hand behind his head, flexing his six-pack when she returned. Damn, he's fine, she thought as she swayed over to him. He pulled back the covers so she could slide right in.

Their lips locked and they held each other tightly. He rolled over on his back, pulling her on top, letting his hand travel down to her ass. He massaged her cheeks while she kissed his neck, face and chest wildly. He moaned while she grunted, both sounding like animals.

She seized his arms and put them up toward the headboard. His body went into submission, letting her take control. She ran her tongue from his forehead all the way down to his hairy pelvis. She held his dick with her tiny, warm hand, stroking it while she kissed the surrounding area. Lifting his balls, she planted a kiss between them and his asshole.

R. Kelly sang, "I feel sooo...freaky tonight. And I need some-one...to make me feel alright." Then the beat came on.

Suddenly, she stopped and came up for air. She sat up on top of him, then took off the chemise. Her titties bounced slightly as she threw it toward the rocking chair. He could feel her pussy's nectar, oozing through her thong. Grabbing hold of her hand-sized titties, she massaged them.

"Have you ever had some Dallas pusssyyy?" she sang, moving her hips in a circular motion.

He flipped her over on her back and repeated the same process she performed. He slid two fingers inside of her while he kissed her inner thighs. She tried to guide his face to her pussy. He tricked her like he was about to do it, then he kissed her on the crack, just below it. Frustration had her constantly trying to find his juicy lips with her pussy, but he kept ducking and dodging her attempts. Two could play that game.

One thing he noticed while he kissed her was that her skin had its own, yet familiar, taste to it. Tired of the foreplay, he pulled off her thong and spread her legs. Just as he was about to enter her, she placed both of her hands on his stomach, stopping him.

"What's wrong?" he asked.

"We can't do it on the first night," she said, panting.

"What?" he hollered, then caught himself. "What you mean?" he said, a little softer this time.

She pulled him down on top of her. "I just wanna be held by you, baby," she said softly. "Just hold me. We ain't gotta be in a rush." Her titties pressed up against his chest as she squeezed him tightly.

A smile appeared on her face after she felt him squeeze her back. She liked him a lot, but she wasn't gonna change the way that she did things for nobody. Her magic had worked on everybody else. Why wouldn't it work on him, too? She wanted to see how much of a player he really was. If she could hook him like she did with every other guy who crossed her path, then she was gonna use him like Goldie. One thing she was sure of, no nigga on this earth would ever make a fool out of Misty Munsey. At one time KC may have owned her heart, but she always got what was coming to her out of him.

Keith could see the game that she was playing. She was a lady and she wanted to be treated like one. He could respect her for that. He'd chill out and play the gentleman role, for now. But she would pay later.

Von Diesel

CHAPTER TWENTY

For the entire week that P'Cola was in Florida, Misty and Keith kicked it together. They went out to clubs, amusement parks, swimming and horseback riding and dined in exotic restaurants. And just like that first time they kicked it together, the nights ended with serious foreplay without going all the way.

He paid for every outing. He even let her talk him into putting a set of spinners on his car. She said it would make him look even sexier when he prowled the streets.

Devontae, Fabien and his mama noticed how distant Keith had been all week. He wouldn't return any of Devontae's phone calls and hadn't stopped by to see his mother. He started showing up for work late and would leave early, before Devontae could get a chance to talk to him.

Fabien had seen Keith and Misty out in traffic, but didn't disturb the two lovebirds while they were spending their quality time together. Since Stacy was out of town with P'Cola, Fabien started spending more time at his office. He was falling for Stacy as well; that's why he didn't blame Keith for spending so much time with Misty. There's always that one special girl who can touch a man's heart, no matter how much of a player he claimed to be.

Even Kylie had gotten the 411 on her friend and ex-lover. It didn't come as a shock; she saw it coming long ago. From the first time that she introduced them, she knew they were attracted to each other. The bad thing about it was that she was still deeply in love with Keith. Plus, they were about to share a bond that could not be broken until death, but she could never catch up with him to discuss it.

Devontae became frustrated with all of his friends. Keith didn't kick it with him. P'Cola didn't kick it with Keith. He was Fabien and Stacy creeping one night, so Fabien avoided P'Cola whenever possible. Everything was going to shit. The very same thing that had motivated them to be the players that they were was coming between them.

***

Keith returned home from a very profitable day at work. He took a cold shower, then fixed himself something to eat. Before he sat down, he pushed play on his answering machine so he could hear his messages.

Natalie had called for the fiftieth time, apologizing for the way she acted at the club that night. Roseshell had called for the sixtieth time, wanting to know where he had been and why she hadn't heard from him. Pam called to see how he was doing. Some unknown person kept calling and hanging up. He figured that someone to be Jamell, still mad at him. Then Pam called again saying that she had graduated from nursing school, and she was officially a Registered Nurse.

There were no more messages. Misty hadn't called since P'Cola had gotten back from Florida, and he still hadn't fucked her.

He flipped through the channels until he found BET. It just so happened that *"The Mack"* was on. Right away he began to think about the first night he and Misty spent together. He thought he had it figured out. She was playing the role of The Mack, and he was Chico, the girl who got mad at Goldie inside the restaurant because he was spending her money on that white girl. Misty may not have spent her money, but he knew that she was spending her time with P'Cola. He had to laugh at the jealous thought.

He heard a car pull up in front of his house, then a door slam. Setting his fork down on his plate, he got up to look out the front door. Peeking out, he saw a face he recognized.

He snatched open the door. "What?" he said harshly. It was Nathalie.

"Can I come in?" She noticed the knot on his head but fought back to urge to look at it.

"Look, bitch," he snapped. "Stay the fuck away from me. If you come around this muthafucka again, I swear I'ma beat the shit out of you."

Her face balled up. "Do it now, pussy," she said, rushing him.

He backed up so he could come in out of the neighbors' view. She swung her small fists wildly. He grabbed her arms. slinging her over the couch. She flipped and hit her head up against the table. Before she knew it, he had one hand around her throat and smacking her hard across the face with the other.

Smack! "You stupid-ass-bitch!" he yelled. Smack! Smack!

"Okay, Ke...ith," she cried. Her lip and nose were both bleeding.

"Not, it ain't okay." Snatching her up, he pushed her into the kitchen. Bent over the counter, she coughed and gasped for air. Keith took a knife out of the dish rack. Twisting her hair in his hand, he pulled her back to him, exposing her throat, then put the knife up to it.

"Bitch, you bet not breathe," he said, barely moving his lips.

She was shaking, crying and trying hard not to swallow. "Kei-"

"Shut up! You ain't so tough now, are you bitch?"

"Pl...ease, don't-__"

"Bitch, I said shut the fuck up. I'm a teach yo' ass a lesson." He dragged her through the house, all the way to the bathroom. He tossed the knife into the face bowl, but kept his grip in her hair.

She screamed loudly in pain and agony. "Please stop! I promise I'll leave you alone," she pleaded. He pulled on her hair. "Ahhhhh!"

"Bending over the bathtub, he turned on the hot water. Forcefully, he put the top part of her head under the running faucet.

"Ahhh--" Some of the very warm water ran into her nose and mouth. She could feel the water on her scalp getting hotter by the second.

"Keith, please. Stop, please!" she begged.

He shut the water off before it got burning hot. As soon as he released his grip, she jumped up, screaming. She slipped on the wet floor but quickly regained her balance on her way to, and out of, the front door.

"Good riddance!" Keith yelled.

"That pussy tried to kill me," she said hoarsely to no one in particular. Climbing into the driver's seat of her F-150, she put it in drive and sped away.

Keith sat back down and began to finish his now cold dinner.

***

Later that night, Keith pulled out of the club parking lot. He had gone to happy hour and had a few drinks to help clear his ahead about what he had done earlier. To validate his actions, he kept telling himself that the bitch had it coming.

After leaving the club, he turned off of Water Street and hopped on the Interstate, going north. The powerful V8 engine was accelerating fast as he eased his foot down on the pedal.

Misty had his head fucked up. The bitch was playing him like he did other bitches. When did shit like that start happening to him? It never did, until Misty. Eventually, he would get over the fact that he'd played the fool, but she was contagious, and he couldn't pull himself away. His thoughts were interrupted by his cell phone vibrating. "Hello," he said somberly.

"Hi, stranger," Misty said in her usual sexy voice.

"Stranger, huh?" He tried to hide the frustration in his voice. "Ain't you one to talk?"

She chuckled. "You mad at me, baby?"

"Nah, I ain't mad. Why should I be mad?" He got into the left lane, then slowed down to the speed limit.

"Because I haven't called." In truth, Misty not calling didn't have anything to do with P'Cola being back in town. After they had spent that week together, she wanted him to crave her. Just to make sure that he was feenin' for only her touch, she would park in front of his house late at night to see if he would call another one of his women over after he didn't hear from her. If he did, they never showed. She knew right then that she had a new fish caught on her hook.

He heard a police siren going off behind him. Glancing in his rearview mirror, he saw a blue police car all up on his bumper.

"Damn!"

"What's wrong, baby?" she said with concern in her voice.

"I'm being pulled over." He got off on the Dauphin Street exit, then pulled over in a McDonald's parking lot.

"What did you do?" she asked curiously.

"Ain't no telling about these cocksuckers out here. I'm on Dauphin Street."

"I'll call back and check on you in a few. Don't call my phone."

"A'ight." Through the mirror, he saw two policemen coming his way.

"Shut off the engine," the shorter of the two ordered.

He did as he was told.

The taller one asked him to step out of the car and produce some identification. He gave them his driver's license. Leaning back against the door of his car, he waited patiently while they ran his name through the computer.

The short office found it amusing that his wheels were spinning while his car was in park.

"Cool," the officer found it amusing that his wheels were spinning while his car was in park.

"No. I'm a car salesman," he replied, emphasizing salesman. He thanked God that he left his gun at home and prayed that they wouldn't smell the alcohol on his breath.

The tall officer removed a pair of handcuffs from his belt, walking toward Keith. "Turn around and put your hands behind your back, please."

"What I---"

"Now!" he yelled. The short officer stepped up, just in case the prisoner tried to resist.

Keith cooperated. They cuffed him and put him in the back seat of their police car.

"What are y'all gonna do with my car?"

"I would think that you would want us to tow it."

"Yeah," the tall officer said. "

Those wheels are way too expensive for us to leave unattended. Car salesman."

***

Stacy was out bowling with some friends. At least that's what she told P'Cola. She was really somewhere laid up with Fabien. So P'Cola picked up a bag of Indo and a bottle of Remy, then headed over to Misty's. He was sitting on her couch, playing football on the Xbox, when the telephone rang.

"I'll get it," she yelled from the kitchen.

"No, I got it," P'Cola said, reaching for the phone. "I'm waiting on a call."

Misty picked up the phone right before he said, "Hello." She remained silent while she listened in on his conversation.

"Wha'sup, P'Cola? This Wayne, nigga?"

"I know who it is," P'Cola said smartly. "Wha'sup Wayne?"

"I need a whole one."

"Shid, you know it's kinda dry out here right now," he said in a low voice. He set the controller down. "So I'ma need twenty-three for it. That's cool?"

"I guess so. You want me to meet you on Clay Street?"

"No, I got a couple of 'em out in my truck. I'm downtown at Misty's. Out there where you saw my truck parked at that time."

"I know where you're at."

"Call me when you get close by. I'll meet you outside. She doesn't need to know my business."

"Bet that." All three of them hung up.

Misty walked into the living room and took a seat beside him. His cell phone began vibrating on the coffee table.

"Hello," he said, answering it.

"P'Cola, this Keith. I'm in jail, man." He sounded desperate. He called all of his females and didn't receive an answer from any of them. Fabien's voicemail kept coming on, and Devontae was in Las Vegas, Nevada. He didn't want to call his mother from jail unless he had to. P'Cola was his only option.

"What you doing in jail?"

"Misty said, "Who is that?"

"Keith," P'Cola said. "He's in jail."

Keith spoke. "I got into a fight with Natalie earlier today and that funky bitch called the police on me." He signed. "I got plenty of bread at home man. I just need you to post my bond so I can get out.

"How much is it?"

"Two thousand. But it's only four hundred through a bondsman."

P'Cola sucked his teeth and said, "I ain't got it, player." He hung up the phone.

Misty's eyebrows shot up. "Damn. How much was it?"

He shrugged. "A couple grand. Now the nigga wanna be my friend because he needs something. If he's so much of a player, why he ain't got one of them hoes running up there to get him?"

"Who knows," Misty said as she got up to go to her bedroom.

She pulled her small safe out from under her bed. Out of her stash, she took two grand and stuffed it into her pocket. The phone rang as Misty came walking back into the living room. P'Cola picked it up and looked at the caller ID. It was Wayne.

"I'm about to go over to Kylie's baby." she said picking her keys up off the table. "I'll be back in a little while."

"A'ight," he said, then continued talking to Wayne who was four blocks away. P'Cola was glad she was leaving. He hoped she would be gone before Wayne pulled up.

She got into her truck and took off in a hurry. What would be more perfect than her making his bond and being out front waiting when they released him? She would feel better about the way she had been treating him.

Taking out her cell phone, she dialed Kylie's number.

"What?" Kylie answered.

"Don't what me, girl. What's wrong with you?"

"Don't even trip. What do you want?"

"I have a question. What jail would they take you to if you were arrested on Dauphin Street?" Misty listened while Kylie gave her all the information that she needed. She also told her not to call a bondsman, because one way was probably already there.

"Thank you, Kylie."

"If you see Keith any time soon, would you please tell him to call me? It's very important."

"What makes you think that I'm gonna see him?"

"Girl, please. Bye."

***

The guard opened the door to the cell. "Keith Monet."

"Yeah," Keith said, standing up.

"Step out please," the guard instructed him.

"What's going on?"

"Bond has been posted," he said nonchalantly.

"By who?"

"Enough with the questions. Let's go."

When he got to the front desk, he saw Misty standing over by the pay phones, talking to the bondsman. He smiled, happy to see her.

He signed his release papers and received his belongings in a brown paper bag. The bondsman told him not to forget to show up for court and to call if he couldn't make it. They shook hands, and that was it. By then, Misty had gone back to her truck to wait for him.

She was on the phone, talking to P'Cola, when Keith climbed into the passenger seat.

"Alright, baby," she was saying. "I'll see you in a little while. Bye." She hung up. Without looking over, she felt Keith staring at her. "What?"

"You're something else. you know that, don't you?"

She put her index finger up to her lips. "Shh. Let me take you to your house and give you a bath first. Then we can talk about it. Okay."

CHAPTER TWENTY-ONE

"I've got to hurry up and get back home," Stacy said, putting her clothes back on. "I wanna be there before he gets back. Plus, I need to wash this sex smell off of me."

Fabien continued to lie there, wallowing on the spacious hotel bed. "You better hope that he don't come in ready to fuck," he said smiling.

She sat down in a chair and began putting on her socks. "I hope not. I've already cum too many times tonight to even dream about going again. My pussy sore as a muthafucka." She put on her shoes. Besides, I'm sure that Misty gave him enough pussy to last him for a while. Whore."

Fabien laughed. "You ain't got room to talk. You supposed to be at the bowling alley with your friends. Instead you ended up on your back in my hotel room."

She looked at him confusingly. Her eyes remained on him while she stood up, walked over to the bed, then lay down beside him.

Rubbing his hard abs, she said, "Thought you said you love me?"

"I do." He kissed her cheek. "But that doesn't change the fact that you got a man."

She rolled over on top of him, then licked his nose. "What if me and P'Cola broke up?"

He frowned. "Look, baby. Just because we're doing our thing don't mean I want to come between you and P'Cola. He's still a friend of mine." He got out the bed and started putting on his clothes. Please don't create any bullshit between me and him."

Stacy sneered at him. "But you love me," She grunted. "Yeah, right." She got up off the bed, picked up her purse, then stormed out the door.

Her cell phone rang as she was pulling out of the parking lot. Fabien's number showed up on the caller ID.

"What you want, P'Cola's friend," she said, answering the phone.

"Baby, why are you acting like that?"

A white Honda Accord ran a stop sign, almost striking the side of Stacy's car. "Fucking' bitch!" she yelled. "God, these people can't drive." She shook her head. "Now what were you saying?"

"All I was trying to say, before you stormed off, was that it would be different if y'all just happened to break up for a different reason. Like if he went to jail or got killed. Don't leave him because of me. You understand what I'm saying?"

"I do, but...I don't know, man. I'm a little confused right now. Look, I'ma call you tomorrow. Okay?"

"You mad?"

"I'm fine. I just need to take the time to figure out what I want to do." Mary J. Blige's *Drama* came on the radio. She turned up the volume a little. "You never know, me and him might work things out."

"A'ight. Call me."

"Bye." She hung up.

With P'Cola, Stacy knew that he could and would give her everything she wanted. With Fabien, things could be the same. The question was, would they? Was he really in love with her or just in lust? If she gambled on love, and lost, she would lose everything. If she won, it would be all good. She chose her third option, which was staying with P'Cola, kicking it with Fabien on the side and putting the rest into God's hands. Damn, she thought, life is a bitch.

Fabien sat in his whip, watching a blue TV screen on one of his six TVs. Instead of pulling off, he sat back in his seat to think for a minute. Things were getting out of hand. He should have never told her that he loved her. That wasn't nothing but his dick talking.

On the down low was how they were supposed to keep their relationship. Now she was talking like she was ready to leave P'Cola for him, and that wasn't cool. Nobody, not even Keith, knew that Fabien made most of his income by washing P'Cola's drug money through his company. He couldn't take the chance of blowing that for some pussy. So he made up his mind. He was gonna have to let her go.

***

Keith stepped out of the tub after Misty finished washing him up. She handed him a towel and told him that she would be out back on the deck when he was ready to talk. After he finished, he put on a pair of boxers and slipped on his flip-flops.

Misty was leaning up against the wooden rail, looking up at the stars, when he stepped out onto the deck. She had taken her clothes off and put on his robe.

She turned around when she heard his footsteps. That arrogant walk and look that he had vanished. Now he had the look of a mad man, who had been hurt. She could see that he was ailing and could feel his body yearning for hers.

He stopped a few feet away from her.

"Come closer," she said, motioning with her finger. "I got something for you." He took his time approaching her. Impatiently, she grabbed his arm, pulling him toward her. "I missed you, baby." Pulling his head down to hers, she kissed his lips.

Keith untied the robe, then picked her up and set her on the rail. She removed the robe so he could get a good look at what he was finally about to get.

"You plan on teasing me again tonight?" he asked, admiring the view.

She shook her head slowly. "Go 'head and hit it, that's what it's made for."

Using her feet, she pulled his boxers down to his knees. Her legs spread, and he stepped between them. He picked up and slid her down on his hard shaft.

"Umph," she grunted, feeling him deep inside of her. She wrapped her arms around his neck. "Fuck me, baby."

He hit her with slow and hard thrusts while she popped her hips back and forth. Taking his time, he carried her over to the patio table, set her down and continued to dig up in her. She lay back on the table, holding her ankles in the air.

"Mmm...oh...ahhh," she moaned loudly. He put his fingers into her mouth for her to suck on.

He didn't race for a nut like he did with most of his women. Instead, he took his time and relished the tight, warm feeling around his dick.

They couldn't hear it, but Misty's cell phone was ringing and would ring for the next two hours. But she would be too occupied to answer the call.

In a rage, P'Cola threw his cell phone against the wall. He was mad because she wasn't answering her damn phone. About an hour before, he had called Kylie and learned that Misty had never come by her apartment. In fact, she had called trying to get some information on bonding somebody out of jail. P'Cola knew that somebody had to have been Keith.

He couldn't understand it. A house, car and money, what else could he have done? Some women were ungrateful. He felt like the biggest fool. It was his own fault that he thought with the little head instead of the big one. She was in love with him. "Wasn't she? Or was she in love with what he could do for her?

Like the police did in a dope house, he searched her room, looking for nothing in particular. He wanted to see what kind of secrets that she might have been hiding. Nothing incriminating was in the closet, the drawers or behind the TV. The only place left to look was under the bed.

"Un huh," he said, pulling the safe out from under her bed.

It was locked, but he knew how to get into it. He took a butter knife, jammed in between the opening of the safe, then slid it sideways until the latch popped open. He whistled at the contents. There had to be over ten grand inside. He cleaned it out, then pushed the safe back under the bed.

"Bitch, I got a surprise for your trifling ass."

He jumped in his Excursion and headed to Keith's house. He was halfway there when he changed his mind. He made an illegal U-turn, going the other direction. It was bad enough that he had

184

tricked all that money off with her. He would really feel like a fool if he drove around looking for her. But he had to be sure. So he turned back around and headed to Keith's house, once again.

From the corner he could see Misty's truck parked in his driveway. Pulling over down the street, he cut out his lights. Out of the console he took a chrome, snub-nose .357.

"Both of them got me fucked up," he said. He ignored the burning feeling inside his big stomach.

He had just grabbed the door handle when he saw a police car cruising slowly up the block. He let the handle go and started the engine back up. They flashed the spotlight on him but kept on going.

P'Cola silently thanked God. If they would've arrived a minute earlier, they would have seen him get out with the gun in his hand. How would he have explained that?

After he put his gun back up, he pulled away and headed back to his own home. He had a woman at the crib who loved him. He made up his mind to forget about Misty and make things right with Stacy.

He headed down Cody Road, he wondered what he would have done if the police hadn't shown up.

His phone rang. "Hello," he answered.

"Hey, fat daddy," Stacy said.

"Wha'sup, baby?" He tried to hide the anger in his voice.

"I just called to let you know that I was at home."

"Okay. I'll be there in a minute." He hung up.

Stacy was already in the bed when he got home. A quick shit and a shower had him ready to call it a night. He climbed into the bed, snuggling up next to her. Gently he began kissing on her back and neck. She squirmed, then her eyes fluttered open.

Not now, she thought. She could feel his hand traveling down her stomach to her pussy. Reaching under the covers, she found his hand and pushed it away.

"Stop, baby," she whined. "I got to be at the doctor's office early in the morning."

"Come on, babe," he pleaded. "We ain't did it in so long. I forgot what it feels like."

That's your fault, she thought.

He cupped her titty.

"Baby, I said I was tired. Damn," she said, irritated.

P'Cola remembered playing her the same way that night he first fucked Misty. He also remembered why he was playing so sleepy, because he had already been fucked good.

Once Stacy's breathing was deep and steady. P'Cola eased out of the bed and tiptoed over to the dresser to where her purse was sitting. It was already open when he reached in and pulled out her wallet. He saw a Visa, Mastercard, driver's license and Fabien's Savings and Loan business card. What was she doing with his card in her wallet?

He wouldn't have suspected anything, but it was tucked behind her driver's license like she was trying to hide it. Stacy picked up her cell phone and went through her calls. Fabien called her three times and she had called him twice.

The burning feeling returned to his gut. Enraged, he snatched the covers off her. The breeze hit her half-naked body.

"Baby, w---"

"Get up, bitch!" he hollered, snatching her up by her hair.

She had a terrified look on her face. "What I do---" he slapped her across her face, letting her fall into the corner. "Oow!" she cried, holding the side of her face.

"You fuckin' my friend?' he quizzed.

"No, baby," she cried. "I wo--"

He snatched her up by her neck, pushed her against the wall and started choking her.

"Ple...ease... d...on...t," she said in a strained voice. He squeezed her neck until her face turned red, then let her go. She slid down the wall to the floor, holding her throat, coughing.

Standing over her he said, "I gave you a house, car, money and this is how you pay me back?" Breathing hard, he turned and walked off, shaking his head unbelievingly.

186

She rose to her feet, then went after him. Just as he was about to walk out the front door, she yelled, "P'Cola. Please don't leave me, baby! I only did it because you fucked that bitch in our house!"

He stopped. He believed her. She got her ass kicked because she had given him a taste of his own medicine. Now that very bitch that he let wreck his home was busy lying on her back in his friend's bed. His love life had gone from sugar to shit real fast. And it was all because of Misty.

"Call Fabien and end it," he said in a low voice. "Don't tell him that I know. Just end it." With that, he walked out the door.

To Be Continued...
Mob Town 2
Coming Soon

Submission Guideline

Submit the first three chapters of your completed manuscript to ldpsubmissions@gmail.com, subject line: Your book's title. The manuscript must be in a .doc file and sent as an attachment. Document should be in Times New Roman, double spaced and in size 12 font. Also, provide your synopsis and full contact information. If sending multiple submissions, they must each be in a separate email.

Have a story but no way to send it electronically? You can still submit to LDP/Ca$h Presents. Send in the first three chapters, written or typed, of your completed manuscript to:

LDP: Submissions Dept
Po Box 944
Stockbridge, Ga 30281

DO NOT send original manuscript. Must be a duplicate.

Provide your synopsis and a cover letter containing your full contact information.

Thanks for considering LDP and Ca$h Presents.

Coming Soon from Lock Down Publications/Ca$h Presents

BOW DOWN TO MY GANGSTA

By **Ca$h**

TORN BETWEEN TWO

By **Coffee**

THE STREETS STAINED MY SOUL **II**

By **Marcellus Allen**

BLOOD OF A BOSS **VI**

SHADOWS OF THE GAME II

TRAP BASTARD II

By **Askari**

LOYAL TO THE GAME **IV**

By **T.J. & Jelissa**

IF LOVING YOU IS WRONG... **III**

By **Jelissa**

TRUE SAVAGE **VIII**

MIDNIGHT CARTEL IV

DOPE BOY MAGIC IV

CITY OF KINGZ III

By **Chris Green**

BLAST FOR ME **III**

A SAVAGE DOPEBOY III

CUTTHROAT MAFIA III

DUFFLE BAG CARTEL VI

HEARTLESS GOON VI

By **Ghost**

A HUSTLER'S DECEIT III

KILL ZONE **II**

BAE BELONGS TO ME III

Von Diesel

A DOPE BOY'S QUEEN III

By **Aryanna**

COKE KINGS V

KING OF THE TRAP III

By **T.J. Edwards**

GORILLAZ IN THE BAY V

3X KRAZY III

De'Kari

THE STREETS ARE CALLING II

Duquie Wilson

KINGPIN KILLAZ IV

STREET KINGS III

PAID IN BLOOD III

CARTEL KILLAZ IV

DOPE GODS III

Hood Rich

SINS OF A HUSTLA II

ASAD

KINGZ OF THE GAME VI

Playa Ray

SLAUGHTER GANG IV

RUTHLESS HEART IV

By Willie Slaughter

FUK SHYT II

By Blakk Diamond

TRAP QUEEN

RICH $AVAGE II

By Troublesome

YAYO V

GHOST MOB II

Mob Town 251

Stilloan Robinson
CREAM III
By Yolanda Moore
SON OF A DOPE FIEND III
HEAVEN GOT A GHETTO II
By Renta
FOREVER GANGSTA II
GLOCKS ON SATIN SHEETS III
By Adrian Dulan
LOYALTY AIN'T PROMISED III
By Keith Williams
THE PRICE YOU PAY FOR LOVE III
By Destiny Skai
I'M NOTHING WITHOUT HIS LOVE II
SINS OF A THUG II
TO THE THUG I LOVED BEFORE II
By Monet Dragun
LIFE OF A SAVAGE IV
MURDA SEASON IV
GANGLAND CARTEL IV
CHI'RAQ GANGSTAS IV
KILLERS ON ELM STREET IV
JACK BOYZ N DA BRONX II
A DOPEBOY'S DREAM II
By **Romell Tukes**
QUIET MONEY IV
EXTENDED CLIP III
THUG LIFE IV
By **Trai'Quan**

191

Von Diesel

THE STREETS MADE ME III

By **Larry D. Wright**

IF YOU CROSS ME ONCE II

ANGEL III

By **Anthony Fields**

FRIEND OR FOE III

By **Mimi**

SAVAGE STORMS III

By **Meesha**

BLOOD ON THE MONEY III

By J-Blunt

THE STREETS WILL NEVER CLOSE II

By K'ajji

NIGHTMARES OF A HUSTLA III

By King Dream

IN THE ARM OF HIS BOSS

By Jamila

HARD AND RUTHLESS III

MOB TOWN 251 II

By Von Diesel

LEVELS TO THIS SHYT II

By Ah'Million

MOB TIES III

By SayNoMore

BODYMORE MURDERLAND II

By Delmont Player

THE LAST OF THE OGS III

Tranay Adams

FOR THE LOVE OF A BOSS II

By C. D. Blue

192

Available Now

RESTRAINING ORDER **I & II**
By **CA$H & Coffee**
LOVE KNOWS NO BOUNDARIES **I II & III**
By **Coffee**
RAISED AS A GOON I, II, III & IV
BRED BY THE SLUMS I, II, III
BLAST FOR ME I & II
ROTTEN TO THE CORE I II III
A BRONX TALE I, II, III
DUFFLE BAG CARTEL I II III IV V
HEARTLESS GOON I II III IV V
A SAVAGE DOPEBOY I II
DRUG LORDS I II III
CUTTHROAT MAFIA I II
By **Ghost**
LAY IT DOWN **I & II**
LAST OF A DYING BREED I II
BLOOD STAINS OF A SHOTTA I & II III
By **Jamaica**
LOYAL TO THE GAME I II III
LIFE OF SIN I, II III
By **TJ & Jelissa**
BLOODY COMMAS I & II
SKI MASK CARTEL I II & III
KING OF NEW YORK I II,III IV V

THE HEART OF A GANGSTA I II& III

By **Jerry Jackson**

CUM FOR ME I II III IV V VI VII

An **LDP Erotica Collaboration**

BRIDE OF A HUSTLA **I II & II**

THE FETTI GIRLS **I, II& III**

CORRUPTED BY A GANGSTA I, II III, IV

BLINDED BY HIS LOVE

THE PRICE YOU PAY FOR LOVE I II

DOPE GIRL MAGIC I II III

By **Destiny Skai**

WHEN A GOOD GIRL GOES BAD

By **Adrienne**

THE COST OF LOYALTY I II III

By **Kweli**

A GANGSTER'S REVENGE **I II III & IV**

THE BOSS MAN'S DAUGHTERS I II III IV V

A SAVAGE LOVE **I & II**

BAE BELONGS TO ME I II

A HUSTLER'S DECEIT I, II, III

WHAT BAD BITCHES DO I, II, III

SOUL OF A MONSTER I II III

KILL ZONE

A DOPE BOY'S QUEEN I II

By **Aryanna**

A KINGPIN'S AMBITON

A KINGPIN'S AMBITION **II**

I MURDER FOR THE DOUGH

By **Ambitious**

TRUE SAVAGE I II III IV V VI VII

Von Diesel

DOPE BOY MAGIC I, II, III
MIDNIGHT CARTEL I II III
CITY OF KINGZ I II
By **Chris Green**
A DOPEBOY'S PRAYER
By **Eddie "Wolf" Lee**
THE KING CARTEL **I, II & III**
By **Frank Gresham**
THESE NIGGAS AIN'T LOYAL **I, II & III**
By **Nikki Tee**

By **CATO**

By **Phoenix**
BOSS'N UP **I , II & III**
By **Royal Nicole**
I LOVE YOU TO DEATH
By Destiny J
I RIDE FOR MY HITTA
I STILL RIDE FOR MY HITTA
By **Misty Holt**

By **Qay Crockett**

SINS OF A HUSTLA
By **ASAD**
BROOKLYN HUSTLAZ
By **Boogsy Morina**
BROOKLYN ON LOCK I & II
By **Sonovia**

196

GANGSTA CITY

By **Teddy Duke**

A DRUG KING AND HIS DIAMOND I & II III

A DOPEMAN'S RICHES

HER MAN, MINE'S TOO I, II

CASH MONEY HO'S

THE WIFEY I USED TO BE I II

By Nicole Goosby

TRAPHOUSE KING **I II & III**

KINGPIN KILLAZ I II III

STREET KINGS I II

PAID IN BLOOD **I II**

CARTEL KILLAZ I II III

DOPE GODS I II

By **Hood Rich**

LIPSTICK KILLAH **I, II, III**

CRIME OF PASSION I II & III

FRIEND OR FOE I II

By **Mimi**

STEADY MOBBN' **I, II, III**

THE STREETS STAINED MY SOUL

By **Marcellus Allen**

WHO SHOT YA **I, II, III**

SON OF A DOPE FIEND I II

HEAVEN GOT A GHETTO

Renta

GORILLAZ IN THE BAY **I II III IV**

TEARS OF A GANGSTA I II

3X KRAZY I II

DE'KARI

Von Diesel

TRIGGADALE I II III

Elijah R. Freeman

GOD BLESS THE TRAPPERS I, II, III

THESE SCANDALOUS STREETS I, II, III

FEAR MY GANGSTA I, II, III IV, V

THESE STREETS DON'T LOVE NOBODY I, II

BURY ME A G I, II, III, IV, V

A GANGSTA'S EMPIRE I, II, III, IV

THE DOPEMAN'S BODYGAURD I II

THE REALEST KILLAZ I II III

THE LAST OF THE OGS I II

Tranay Adams

THE STREETS ARE CALLING

Duquie Wilson

MARRIED TO A BOSS... I II III

By Destiny Skai & Chris Green

KINGZ OF THE GAME I II III IV V

Playa Ray

SLAUGHTER GANG I II III

RUTHLESS HEART I II III

By Willie Slaughter

FUK SHYT

By Blakk Diamond

DON'T F#CK WITH MY HEART I II

By Linnea

ADDICTED TO THE DRAMA I II III

IN THE ARM OF HIS BOSS II

By Jamila

YAYO I II III IV

A SHOOTER'S AMBITION I II

By S. Allen

TRAP GOD I II III

RICH $AVAGE

By Troublesome

FOREVER GANGSTA

GLOCKS ON SATIN SHEETS I II

By Adrian Dulan

TOE TAGZ I II III

LEVELS TO THIS SHYT

By Ah'Million

KINGPIN DREAMS I II III

By Paper Boi Rari

CONFESSIONS OF A GANGSTA I II III

By Nicholas Lock

I'M NOTHING WITHOUT HIS LOVE

SINS OF A THUG

TO THE THUG I LOVED BEFORE

By Monet Dragun

CAUGHT UP IN THE LIFE I II III

By Robert Baptiste

NEW TO THE GAME I II III

MONEY, MURDER & MEMORIES I II III

By **Malik D. Rice**

LIFE OF A SAVAGE I II III

A GANGSTA'S QUR'AN I II III

MURDA SEASON I II III

GANGLAND CARTEL I II III

CHI'RAQ GANGSTAS I II III

KILLERS ON ELM STREET I II III

Von Diesel

JACK BOYZ N DA BRONX

A DOPEBOY'S DREAM

By **Romell Tukes**

LOYALTY AIN'T PROMISED I II

By Keith Williams

QUIET MONEY I II III

THUG LIFE I II III

EXTENDED CLIP I II

By **Trai'Quan**

THE STREETS MADE ME I II

By **Larry D. Wright**

THE ULTIMATE SACRIFICE I, II, III, IV, V, VI

KHADIFI

IF YOU CROSS ME ONCE

ANGEL I II

By **Anthony Fields**

THE LIFE OF A HOOD STAR

By Ca$h & Rashia Wilson

THE STREETS WILL NEVER CLOSE

By K'ajji

CREAM I II

By Yolanda Moore

NIGHTMARES OF A HUSTLA I II

By King Dream

CONCRETE KILLA I II

By Kingpen

HARD AND RUTHLESS I II

MOB TOWN 251

By Von Diesel

GHOST MOB II

Stilloan Robinson
MOB TIES I II
By SayNoMore
BODYMORE MURDERLAND
By Delmont Player
FOR THE LOVE OF A BOSS
By C. D. Blue

Von Diesel

BOOKS BY LDP'S CEO, CA$H

TRUST IN NO MAN

TRUST IN NO MAN 2

TRUST IN NO MAN 3

BONDED BY BLOOD

SHORTY GOT A THUG

THUGS CRY

THUGS CRY 2

THUGS CRY 3

TRUST NO BITCH

TRUST NO BITCH 2

TRUST NO BITCH 3

TIL MY CASKET DROPS

RESTRAINING ORDER

RESTRAINING ORDER 2

IN LOVE WITH A CONVICT

LIFE OF A HOOD STAR

CPSIA information can be obtained
at www.ICGtesting.com
Printed in the USA
LVHW082128120821
695175LV00012B/354